The Last Refuge

MARTIN ROY HILL

32-32 North
San Diego, CA

THE LAST REFUGE
Copyright © 2015 by Martin Roy Hill.

32-32 North

An imprint of
M. R. Hill Publishing
San Diego, California

For information contact
www.martinroyhill.com

Cover photograph by Nico Smit | Dreamstime.com

ISBN-13:978-1518682711

ISBN-10:1518682715

First Edition: January 2016

Books by Martin Roy Hill

Duty: Stories of Mystery and Suspense from the Cold War and Beyond (2012)
The Killing Depths (2012)
Empty Places (2013)
Eden: A Sci-Fi Novella (2014)

"Patriotism is the last refuge of a scoundrel."

Samuel Johnson, 1775

On describing those who hide their greed behind a veil of patriotic fervor.

(Boswell's Life of Johnson)

PROLOGUE

IRAQ, 1991

X-ray One, this is X-ray. Say again."

The radio crackled as the military police lieutenant fingered the mike. "X-ray, X-ray One. I say again. We have a wounded American civilian. Repeat, a wounded American civilian. We need a dust off."

"Roger, X-ray One. Is this a journalist?"

"Negative, X-ray. His papers ID him as an American engineer named Robert Stanning." The officer spelled the name phonetically.

"Was he one of Saddam's guestages?"

X-ray referred to a number of foreigners Iraq's dictator, Saddam Hussein, had taken hostage, hoping to stave off an international military response to his invasion of Iraq's neighbor, Kuwait. Hussein denied the captives were hostages. He called them "guests," and the news media combined the two descriptions into the term 'guestages.'

"Now how the hell would I know that?" the lieutenant said to the driver of the Humvee.

The driver, a young black MP in desert fatigues smiled and shook his head. "Rear echelon mental giants," he said.

"I have no idea, X-ray. He's unconscious. We found him in an Iraqi field hospital near Basra. The Eye-racks just said he was wounded during one of our bombing attacks. He needs a dust off—quick. Over."

"Roger, X-ray One. What's your position?"

The lieutenant studied a field map and sighed. Pinpointing their position in the Iraqi desert would be much easier if they were issued the kind of GPS satellite receivers the Special Forces units had, but regular army units didn't rate them yet. After a few moments, the officer transmitted the estimated coordinates.

"Roger, X-ray One. Standby."

The MP lieutenant listened to the RT crackle some more, tossed the mike onto the dashboard, then picked it up again. "X-ray Two, X-ray One. You there, Alvarez?"

The RT crackled with a voice from the Bradley fighting vehicle following the lieutenant's own Humvee. "Roger, lieutenant."

"How's our passenger?"

"Still unconscious, lieutenant." After a pause, Alvarez added. "He don't look good."

"X-ray One, X-ray."

The officer thumbed the push-to-talk button. "X-ray One."

"The dust offs are stranded. The juice goose hasn't caught up yet. The closest they can get to you is LZ Zebra. You're going to have to hotfoot it to them. Over."

"Roger, X-ray." The lieutenant picked up the map again, folded it over and found Landing Zone Zebra penciled in. "I have the coordinates, X-ray. We're en route. X-ray One out."

The lieutenant settled back in the Humvee's front passenger seat. "We're moving forward so fast, the logistics tail can't keep up. The choppers don't have enough fuel up forward to fly out to us. We have to go to them."

"Someone ought to tell those Eye-racks to put up more of a fight." The driver shook his head and clucked.

The officer grimaced. "Funny, Mitchell. Funny as a Scud. Let's go."

The lieutenant peered into the darkness outside the Humvee. Night in the Iraqi desert was an odd experience of total isolation amid massive congestion. The sky was as black as oil. In fact, it virtually was oil, with thick swirling black clouds of smoke thrown up by Kuwait's burning oil fields hiding the heavens. Behind the Humvee, the lightless Bradley melted into the darkness, only its engine noise revealing its presence. In the distance behind them, was the sound of cannon fire.

They drove on, guided only by the feel of the road.

The first spasms of diarrhea began to cramp the officer's intestinal track. "Damn. God damn it to hell."

"Lieutenant?"

"I've got the damn trots again, Mitchell. Pull up before I shit in my pants."

The Humvee slowed to a stop. "I told you not to eat that street food back in Saudi."

"Shut up, Mitchell." The lieutenant opened the Humvee's door and climbed out. "Radio the Bradley to slow down. We don't want them to ram into us in this dark." The lieutenant disappeared into the shadows.

"Roger that."

§

In the dark, Alvarez could just make out the dim outline of the Humvee. He pulled the Bradley up alongside. Behind him, in the cargo bay, a voice hollered, "Lieutenant better not take too long. I don't think this guy's gonna last."

"Vaccaro, when you gotta go, you gotta go," Alvarez said. "Know what I mean?"

In the Humvee, Mitchell was just as anxious. With the lieutenant gone, he suddenly felt terribly isolated. He opened the door on his side and stepped out. Looking around, his hand automatically groped for his M-16 rifle.

"Mitch." The radio crackled with Alvarez's voice. "Is the lieutenant back yet?"

Mitchell reached down into the cab and picked up the mike. "That's a negative."

"I don't feel too good sitting out here like this," Alvarez said. "I got hair on my neck bristling."

Neither Mitchell nor Alvarez heard the muffled motors of the Cobra attack helicopters. A flash of light caught Mitchell's eye, then he saw the long yellow streak of a missile. "INCOMING!" he screamed into the mike. The missile slammed into the Humvee before he could say any more. The blast of its armor-piercing warhead tore the top of the vehicle off, and left the vehicle lying on its side, burning.

Even before the Humvee settled from the blast, a second missile slammed into the Bradley. Its warhead burned into the Bradley's armor with a jet of molten metal and exploded, turning the fighting vehicle into a cauldron of flaming death.

The gunships screamed over the carnage they had wreaked. The pilot of the lead ship looked out his window at the two burning vehicles. In the light of the flames, he recognized the familiar shape of the Bradley and the glint of an inverted "V" on its side, the recognition symbol for the Coalition Forces. The pilot felt his insides go empty.

"Oh, shit," was all he could say.

CHAPTER 1

San Diego, California

1993

It was pure coincidence I happened to be in the P.R. director's office when Jack Sweeney went off the roof top and ended his sorry little existence ten floors below. The director, David Brooks, was already nervous talking to me about another company death. His demeanor was professional, his speech cool and reserved. His hands didn't even sweat much. Yet his eyes flitted skittishly around the room as we talked, never once landing on mine.

Brooks' professional demeanor became as fidgety as his eye movements when an assistant burst into his office and shouted: "Jack Sweeney just jumped off the roof!"

"What?" Brooks' chair flew backward and he was on his feet doing a little pirouette. He rushed to the window and looked down, saw nothing, and rushed to another window outside his private office. I followed a few leisurely seconds later.

An office full of rubberneckers crowded around the huge, tinted windows, their heads craned downward. Brooks turned and looked at me. His suit coat was buttoned, but his tie had escaped its confines. His hands were sweating badly, and he rubbed them absently against the fine pinstripe of this suit. His eyes finally focused on me, staring like a frightened animal.

"We, ah, seem to have had a terrible tragedy here," he said.

"Jack Sweeney jumped off the roof," I said. Brooks nodded. I'd done my homework on Consolidated Electronics, and knew who Jack Sweeney was. "He's your director of development, isn't he?" A second clicked by and I corrected myself. "Was."

Brooks nodded. "He's been very, ah, depressed since his son was killed in Desert Storm. Very depressed, poor man." Brooks looked back at the window, then at me. "I suppose you'll want to call someone. Your office. Your newspaper, or, rather, your magazine, wasn't it? But, please, no photographs. For the family, you know."

Time was I would have rushed out of the building and pushed my way through police cordons to see the body and take its picture, and damn the family sensitivities. However, I hadn't worked for a newspaper in years, and it had been nearly a year since I left my wire service office in Mexico City and moved back to San Diego to freelance. I could have rushed to my car for my camera and taken some photographs to sell to the local broadsheets. I could have used the money. But I wasn't up to that stuff anymore.

I shook my head. "That's not what I came to talk to you about, Mr. Brooks. Perhaps I should come back at another time, when things calm down."

The P.R. director looked relieved. "Certainly, Mr. Brandt. Certainly. Anytime." He started showing me out the door, then paused. "And thank you."

He turned and went into his office. The last glimpse I had of David Brooks, he was talking on the phone.

§

It had been a week since Tom Collier called me into to his office at *San Diego Life* and told me about his old girlfriend. I knew Tom from my days covering the area for my wire service, before I headed south. He was executive editor of the magazine, a short rotund man with a cherubic face anchored by a bushy moustache and topped by hair as thick and as wild as his moustache. By his own admission, Tom was a lousy editor. He preferred leaving the word work to the magazine's other staffers. Still, Tom knew everyone in town, and if San Diego had a pulse, Tom's stubby little finger was on it.

"I've got this old girlfriend, Pete," Tom said. "She's kind of in trouble. I told her I'd help her out."

"We're into playing Don Quixote these days?" I asked.

Tom shook his head. "No, nothing like that. This is a legit story. She'd like to see some press coverage of it, and I told her I'd see to it."

I raised my eyebrows but said nothing.

"See, she's got this lawsuit against the government and ConEl."

Tom dug through the papers on his desk until he found a stapled bundle about a fourth of an inch thick, and handed it to me. It was a complaint filed in U.S. District Court against the U.S. Marine Corps and Consolidated

Electronics. I started skimming the pages, but Tom stopped me.

"Just let me brief you first," he said. "This old girlfriend, her name's Susan, Susan Stanning . . ."

"The plaintiff."

"Yeah. Sue's husband was killed in one of those 'friendly fire' incidents in the Gulf War and—"

"He was GI?"

"No, a civilian," Tom answered. "An engineer with ConEl." I started to ask another question, but Tom raised a hand. "That's it. Just bear with me. This guy was found by some army unit in an Iraqi medical station near . . ." Tom waved his hand trying to catch the name, then gave up. "Anyway, near some camel-rider city there in Iraq. He'd been wounded by our bombing, and this army unit was taking him to one of our hospitals or something when a Marine helicopter blew them up thinking they were Iraqis."

"What was her husband doing there? I thought Hussein released all of the civilian hostages before the fighting started."

"He wasn't a hostage."

This time I let him continue without interruption.

"That's why Sue's suing ConEl. She wants to know why her husband was in Iraq instead of Germany where he told her he would be. She wants to know why this Marine whirlybird suddenly appeared out of nowhere and blew up the army guys taking him back to safety."

"What has ConEl told her? Or the government?"

"Not a damn thing, Pete. Not a damn thing. ConEl said they didn't know why he was in Iraq. Denied knowing anything about it. They said Sue's husband wasn't even working for them at the time. And the government just says it was a terrible accident and to forget about it. Get on with her life."

"So she filed a lawsuit?"

"Right. And now the government and ConEl are trying to suppress the suit. They're saying she can't sue the government or ConEl—ConEl because it was acting as an agent of the government during the war."

"An agent of the government?"

"We have no idea what that means. There's more. The government pleaded for a gag order on this whole case, and got it. That's why Sue came to me. She hopes if the press gets wind of this thing, it might force the government to own up."

"Your girlfriend's already in violation of the gag order." I waved the complaint.

"She has no idea where that came from, nor do I. Know what I mean?"

"Just appeared in the mail, no return address, right?" I suggested.

Tom smiled. "An anonymous tip."

"There's one problem, Tom," I said. "A story like this could take weeks to develop. I can't afford to spend that much time on a story for the rates you pay."

I expected Tom to be miffed, or at least hurt. Instead, he grinned like the Cheshire Cat.

"I have a special fund I keep in reserve for special stories. I can give you three grand for the piece, plus reasonable expenses. And you have only three weeks to get it in."

"You're taking quite a chance," I said. "Must be quite a lady."

"She was the love of my life," Tom said gravely.

"Every woman you know is the love of your life," I said.

"Okay, put it this way," he answered, grinning. "She's single again."

CHAPTER 2

I read the complaint sitting in my doctor's lobby. It charged ConEl, the Marine Corps, the army, Defense Department, and the U.S. government in general with virtually every cause of action Susan Stanning's attorney could think of, from breach of contract to negligence. Yet what I read did little to add to what Tom Collier told me.

Robert Stanning was 47 years old, an electronics engineer born in Bonn, Germany, but naturalized in the U.S. when he was 35. He was employed by ConEl for ten years, most recently holding the position of field representative. That position kept him traveling much of the time. In early December 1990, Stanning told his wife he had to fly to Germany on business. He expected to be back in time for Christmas. A week before Christmas, he called and said he wouldn't be home until after New Year's. On New Year's Day, he called his wife one last time, saying he should be home within a week.

For the next six weeks, Susan Stanning heard nothing from or about her husband. Calls to ConEl only heightened her fear when she was told Stanning hadn't worked for the company for at least a year. Calls to the

State Department and the American Embassy in Germany provided no relief; according to German records, Stanning never entered the country. The next time she heard about Robert Stanning, it was in a cable from the State Department saying he had died in an Iraqi hospital near Basra of wounds apparently inflicted by Allied bombing.

No doubt that came as a shock to the widow Stanning, but not as much as what came next. Stanning's body arrived in a closed coffin. Susan Stanning demanded a medical examiner autopsy her husband's body to determine his cause of death, only to discover his body was burned beyond recognition and shredded by shrapnel.

The final shock came when Stanning's few surviving personal effects arrived with an army graves registration form listing the cause of death as "fratricide," or friendly fire. The form also listed a date and a location that didn't quite jibe with what the State Department claimed.

The complaint alleged Stanning had been to Iraq on business for ConEl several times over the past few years. That he was found in Iraq by army troops indicated he was there again on business for the company, the suit concluded.

I put the complaint down and rubbed my eyes. I thought it unlikely Stanning was back in Iraq on business; most foreign companies started pulling their people out of the country after Saddam Hussein marched into Kuwait. Those who remained became the dictator's "guests." Thousands of foreign nationals, among them American, British, and French engineers who had helped build Baghdad's massive war machine, were held hostage for weeks. All were eventually released, and Stanning was not among them. So why was he in Basra?

A nurse interrupted my thinking and led me into an examination room to await the doctor. The smell of antiseptic was strong and the room's white walls looked too sterile. The doctor was a short blond man with sun-bleached hair who looked too young to have already completed medical school and a residency. But he had been treating my headaches for months now, and I had to admit they were getting better.

He checked my blood pressure, my eyes, and my reflexes, then probed the scar that ran from my nose through the right eyebrow. The scar was placed there a few years earlier by the rifles of Salvadoran soldiers who didn't like me taking their photograph while they butchered a young peasant woman and her baby.

"Does it still hurt to the touch?" he asked.

"Not really," I said. "It still throbs when I get a headache, though."

He grunted and checked my file. "Is the medicine helping?"

I nodded. "And it doesn't make me sick like the codeine the Mexican doctors gave me."

"I should think not," the young doctor said. "You still smoking?"

"Quit."

"Drinking?"

"Cut back."

"Good. What about sleeping?"

I shook my head. "I'm still having nightmares."

The doctor closed my file and looked at me. "I'm sorry," he said. "That's something I can't really help you with. I'm sure they'll go away with time. Have you thought about seeing a therapist?"

§

The doctor's receptionist wrote out the name and number of a psychiatrist on a referral card, which I stuck in my wallet and left there. I had other things on my mind than to share my ghosts with a stranger. I was driving an old Mustang then, and I turned it toward downtown and headed for the Federal Building.

The closest place I found to park was in a pay lot four blocks from the Fed Building. It took 15 minutes to walk through the city traffic to the massive black office structure straddling two blocks along Broadway in the heart of Centre City. Remnants of yellow ribbons hung dismally from lampposts along Broadway, reminders of the homecoming parade the city held months before for veterans of the Persian Gulf War.

It was warm for a winter day and I felt sweat trickle down my sides. I took my sports jacket off and slowed my pace, marvelling at how my blood had thickened since coming back north.

A federal security officer at the entrance waved a metal detector at me before motioning me inside. The clerk's office for the U.S. District Court was down a long corridor on the ground floor. I wanted to check the court files for the Stanning lawsuit. Even with a gag order, a case file usually contained papers not covered by the order, papers that could lead to places or persons, or simply other pieces of paper.

I had the case number from the complaint, but out of habit I checked the microfiche index, found the case listed, and wrote down the number on a request slip. A cherubic Latina clerk with large dark eyes and an infectious smile took it and returned minutes later, her smile less infectious.

"Kind of thin, isn't it?" she said.

Thin it was. Inside was a single sheet of paper, a case status form indicating all documents connected with the case were sealed by order of the court. The sheet didn't even mention the names of the plaintiff or the defendants.

"This is all there was?" The clerk nodded. "There's no other folder?" She shook her head.

"Kind of strange, huh?"

"Yeah," I said, handing the folder back. "Kind of strange."

I stood at a bank of elevators, leaning on the button and mulling over just how strange it really was. The elevator ride to the top floor offices of the U.S. Attorney was slow and suffocating, with lawyers and defendants crowding into the car at each landing. I shoved my business card through a hole in the bulletproof glass and told the receptionist I needed to talk to her public information officer. The receptionist took the card, smiled tightly and picked up the phone. The glossy red polish on her nails caught the light, but nothing like the rock that flashed on her ring finger.

She hung up the phone and smiled at me again. "Mr. Aiken will be with you shortly."

"Thank you. That's a gorgeous engagement ring. When's the happy day?"

"Isn't it?" She beamed as she held the diamond closer to the glass for me to see. "The wedding's next week. This is my last day here." She giggled, then admired the ring herself.

"Leaving?"

"Why not? My fiancé's a defense attorney. With his income, we don't need mine."

The receptionist smiled proudly. Now it was my turn to smile tightly.

"Shortly" turned into a fifteen-minute wait. Aiken shoved through the heavy security door like a defensive lineman which—judging by his girth—he probably was in college. He straightened the collar on his pinstripe jacket, offered me a thick hand, and introduced himself.

"George Aiken, special prosecutor and part-time PIO. What can I do for you Mr.—" He glanced at my card in his left hand. "Mr. Brandt?"

I told him I was doing a story on ConEl and understood a suit was naming them and the U.S. government as defendants. I told him I found the suit in the court clerk's index, but the folder was empty, the file sealed by the court. "I was just interested in knowing if there was anything at all you could tell me about the suit," I concluded.

Aiken's mouth tugged at the corners. "I know nothing about it," he said. "You got the case number? I can look it up, maybe find you someone who knows what it's about. But if it's sealed, we won't be able to tell you much."

"I understand." I copied the number onto a blank page in my notebook and tore the page out, handing it to Aiken before he disappeared behind the heavy security door.

It was another fifteen minutes before Aiken returned. His face was tight and red, and sweat beaded above his collar. His jaw muscles flexed nervously.

"I sorry, Mr. Brandt, but you must be mistaken," he said. "There's no such case."

"That can't be," I said. "I just saw the case folder."

"We have no record of such a lawsuit filed against the United States government. I personally checked with the clerk's office downstairs and they said no such case exists. Are you certain this is the case number?"

I compared the number I gave him with the one in my notebook. "That's the number."

"Well, like I said then, you must be mistaken."

Before I could stammer out a protest, Aiken disappeared behind the security door. I glanced at the receptionist, but she was busy showing her ring to another woman in her cubicle.

I rode the elevator down to the first floor and hurried to the clerk's office. I checked each of the microfiche cardholders, but the card with the Stanning case number was gone in every one. I filled out another request slip and handed it to the same Latina clerk.

"You again?" she said smiling. "Isn't this the same number?"

"Yeah," I answered, trying hard to keep my voice civil. "I just wanted to take another look at that empty file."

The clerk shrugged and disappeared behind the file racks. Five minutes later, I was still standing at the counter, growing more impatient. A balding man in a three-piece pinstripe and wingtips strode up to the counter and handed me my request slip.

"I'm sorry, sir, but there is no case with this number,' he said. He had the bearing and manner of a schoolmaster.

"What the hell do you mean there's no such case?" I slapped the request slip down in front of him. "I was looking at the case file here just half an hour ago."

The man pinched his nose, drew an impatient breath, then looked at me as if he were addressing a naughty child. "I'm sorry, sir, there is no such case. Perhaps you would like to check the index again?"

"The damn microfiche with that case number was taken away. It was here half an hour ago, too."

The schoolmaster shook his head, lips pursed. "I simply don't know what you mean, sir."

CHAPTER 3

I stood outside the government building breathing hard and deep to control my anger. I reached into my pocket for a cigarette, and remembered the pack was no longer there. That only made me madder.

The anger on my face as I marched back to my car was so apparent even the panhandlers didn't look my way. Obviously, the USA's office was stonewalling me. But why? What was it about the Stanning suit that would make the government deny its very existence?

Wheeling out of the paid lot, I wended my way through downtown's one-way streets until I caught the I-5 and headed north. It was late afternoon, and the low sun glinted off the jets taking off from Lindbergh Field and, a little beyond, off the placid waters of Mission Bay. Twenty minutes later, I parked in one of the lots at the university in La Jolla, tossed a press permit on the dash, and walked across campus to the library.

It was winter, but you couldn't tell that by the way the students dressed. Young women strolled the walkways in shorts and blouses, cradling their books close to their chests. A blonde in stretchy bicycle shorts and a halter-top glided by on a ten-speed, her hair flowing behind her. Something screeched behind me. I turned and watched a youth with a scraggly beard and baggy shorts and T-shirt do a 360 on a skateboard before banking to his left and scooting past me.

The university library was a model of experimental architecture. It crouched on a grassy campus knoll like an alien spacecraft, a whitewashed jumble of cantilevered right angles. I'd been using its facilities since the public library downtown had become a day care center for the city's homeless. Inside, undergrads crowded around the computer terminals and I had to wait for one to open up. I used the time to make a call to David Needles, Susan Stanning's attorney.

Needles' receptionist was polite but succinct. Mr. Needles was in conference and couldn't be disturbed.

"Furthermore," she continued, "Mr. Needles knows nothing about a Stanning case."

I let that settle into my brain before replying.

"I know he filed a lawsuit complaint for Mrs. Susan Stanning charging the Marine Corps and the U.S. government with negligence in the death of her husband, Robert," I said.

The receptionist's voice sounded strained as she answered. "Mr. Needles knows nothing about such a lawsuit, sir."

I knew a stall when I heard one. I also knew there was nothing I could do about it just then. I thanked the receptionist, left my name and number, and told her I hoped Mr. Needles would reconsider.

A terminal finally opened up. I sat down, drew out my long reporter's notebook and logged into the newspaper database.

There were plenty of stories about ConEl in the local rag. The defense contractor was the city's largest employer. Rather, it had *been* the city's largest employer. Massive cuts in defense spending since the end of the Cold War and, later, the Gulf War had left ConEl with too few contracts to maintain its huge work force. Senior management maneuvered to save their jobs while sacrificing the blue-collar rank-and-file in droves to the bottom line.

The company itself was about to get pink-slipped, too. General Technologies, ConEl's troubled parent company, was being slowly dismembered by its CEO, Thomas T. Hess. Operation Desert Storm provided only temporary relief from the post-Cold War defense drawdown. Thousands of workers were laid off at GT holdings around the country, including ConEl, and unprofitable subsidiaries auctioned off to the highest bidder. With its defense contracts dwindling, rumors flew that ConEl was on the auction block, too. Hess, meanwhile, had given himself a $1.6 million bonus on top of his $2.4 million salary.

Not a bad job, I told myself.

I took it all down in my notebook for background and went further back in the newspaper archives. After another 15 minutes, someone tapped me on the shoulder. I looked up into the pinched face of a coed librarian who looked to be working hard on old-maidenhood.

"Your thirty minutes are up, sir."

I gathered my notes, sat a nearby table and went over them as I waited for a second chance on the terminal.

The 1980s were the defense industry's heyday. Calling them democracy's first line of defense, Ronald Reagan threw money at what his predecessor, Dwight Eisenhower, called the "military industrial complex" like a drunken sailor throwing tips at a stripper. The defense industries responded like sharks to the smell of blood. It was an age of greed and shoddy workmanship, and more than one airman, sailor, or soldier paid the ultimate price in the name of corporate avarice.

GT and ConEl weren't alone in the feeding frenzy, but they were among the largest mouths in the hungry school. Both companies had a long litany of charges pressed against them, from egregious over-billing to criminal fraud. Yet the government continued doing business with them. ConEl's biggest wrist slap was a $500,000 fine for providing the Navy with substandard and untested parts for one of its weapons systems. The company paid the fine, then passed the cost on to the government as a miscellaneous expense. No one noticed until a whistle-blower revealed the fraud years later.

Another terminal opened up and I searched the newspaper database for stories about Gulf War friendly fire incidents. The list of stories the computer found was too long to read in one sitting. The speed of the allied advance and the expanse of the battlefield caused widespread confusion among the Coalition Forces. Friendly fire was epidemic. The allies painted inverted Vs on their vehicles for easier recognition, but it did little to clear what Clausewitz called "the fog of war." I knew that fog well. Down south and in the Gulf, I'd seen firefights where no one was sure whom they were fighting, or if they were fighting anyone at all.

It took five minutes of refining my search before I came up with a list of stories I was able to handle. Out of those, there was one story about an incident matching the events related by the Stanning suit. It told me little more than the complaint did.

Six months earlier, a local radio talk show aired a discussion about friendly fire incidents. The host received a call from a man calling himself Paul, who said he was a Marine Corps chopper pilot. Paul's voice cracked with emotion as he described leading a flight of two Cobra gunships in an attack on what they thought were two Iraqi military vehicles. It was only after the attack he realized they were American vehicles. Later, Paul was told three army MPs died in the attack.

The radio station and the local newspapers tried to confirm Paul's story without luck. As far as the Marines and the Pentagon were concerned, Paul was just a drunk with an overactive imagination.

"Sir, your time is almost up."

I glanced up from my notebook into the pinched face of the librarian. I grinned and held up a finger. "Just one more thing, then I'm out of here."

She pursed her lips and nodded gravely, then walked away. I typed in the name of Susan Stanning's attorney. What I found out about Mr. Needles made me purse my lips. I scribbled some more notes, closed my notebook and headed out. On the way, I winked at the librarian. She did not wink back.

CHAPTER 4

Before leaving the university, I dropped more coins into a pay phone and dialed David Needles again. The receptionist was cooler this time. When she spoke, she pronounced each word as if she thought English was a poor second language to me.

"I told you," she said, "Mr. Needles cannot talk to you about the Stanning case. Mr. Needles cannot even admit there is a Stanning case. He is under court order, sir. Do you understand?"

"Yes, I do," I replied in the same slow, precise manner. "And thank you, miss, for confirming the existence of the case."

"What? But I . . .You don't—"

I interrupted her stammering to leave my name and number again, then hung up. I looked up ConEl's main number in the phone book, and dropped more coins into the phone.

It took a couple of minutes for ConEl's operator to patch me through to the corporate public relations office.

I identified myself to David Brooks and told him I was doing a story for *San Diego Life* on how local defense firms were coping with the Pentagon's spending cuts. Some might call that lying. In my business, we call it pretext.

Brooks' response was magnanimous.

"Great," he said. "Come on down, I'll personally give you the fifty-cent tour. It used to be the dollar tour, but with all the cutbacks we had to cut that, too!" Brooks laughed loudly at his joke.

I asked to come by the next day.

"Fine!" Brooks said. He gave me the time. "I'll leave your name at the main gate. They'll be able to show you where to go."

§

Brooks was good to his word. The uniformed guard at the main gate handed me a map to the public relations office and waved me through as soon as I told him my name.

The ConEl facility sat on more than three city blocks of land on Kearny Mesa. Brooks' office was on the eighth floor of the company's ten story administrative building. The office looked out across a large playing field adjoining the company's employee health club and, beyond that, Interstate 15 and, farther beyond, the new residences of Tierrasanta. Immediately below the PR office stood a full-size mock-up of a ballistic missile.

On the paneled walls of Brooks' office hung photographs of rockets riding fiery tails into the sky, war jets spitting death from mini-guns in their snouts, and satellites wrapped in glistening protective foil made of gold. A massive oak desk matched the paneling on the wall. A thickly padded black leather chair sat askew behind the desk.

"Mr. Brandt?"

David Brooks buttoned his English-cut pinstripe coat, and tugged it straight by the hem. He offered me a finely manicured hand. His smile revealed brilliant capped teeth. His closely trimmed hair had a slight curl to it, with strips of gray running through brown. His handshake was dry but weak.

He offered me a chair that matched the one behind his desk, then sat at his desk, leaning forward, hands clasped and resting on the desk, and smiling expectantly.

"Now, how can I help you?" he asked.

I crossed my legs, adjusted my position in the chair, and smiled back with as much false goodwill as Brooks' smile held.

"As I said on the phone, I just want to know what ConEl is doing to cope with the bad economy and defense cuts. I know you're laying off workers, for instance, but is ConEl attempting to convert its facilities to non-defense product lines? And, if so, how?"

Brooks' hands tightened slightly on the desk. His lips pursed, then he nodded.

"You're absolutely right," he said. "We have been laying employees off. Unfortunate, but necessary. As to the other, the answer is no. We have chosen not to pursue the economic conversion course, as other defense firms have."

"Why is that?"

"America is always going to need a strong defense," Brooks said. "The recent war with Iraq shows that."

He waved his hands toward the photos on his walls. "And we're simply the best in the business at providing it. We and our parent company, General Technologies. It's true we'll never have another era as we did in the Eighties, but we've always known that would eventually end. Now we're downsizing and streamlining our operations to match the new reality, just as we upsized in the last decade to match the reality of that era. But we intend to always be here, Mr. Brandt, for the good of America."

And for your bottom line, I told myself. I scribbled in my notebook.

"I suspect this is a rather touchy subject, the downsizing and all?" I asked.

"Not touchy," Brooks said. "An unfortunate reality of government contract work. But we're proud of the work ConEl does here, and we appreciate the opportunity to show our community we intend to remain a major asset to it."

Brooks watched approvingly as I took notes from his little speech. He stood and stretched an opened hand toward the door.

"Come," he said. "I'll show you our facilities."

I followed Brooks through the outer offices to the elevator, which we rode to the ground floor. He led me through a passage that took us from the admin building to a series of low-slung manufacturing units. The hallways were crowded with workers in suits or jeans, some wearing white lab smocks. In one building, we watched workers assemble a small anti-ship missile. In another, workers in white surgical garb pieced together a satellite in a room kept sterile and dust-free by special environmental controls. After an hour of touring, we ended up in a conference room back in the admin building.

"This is our special pride and joy," Brooks said.

He turned toward the back wall and snapped his fingers. The lights dimmed and the front wall slid back to reveal a large-screen television. The screen snapped alive with an aerial shot of a large transport jet. Sprouting from its dorsal like a huge metal mushroom was a circular radar dome.

"CCOMS," a female narrator's voice boomed from the set. She pronounced it *See-Comms.* "Combat Command Organization and Management System. Consolidated Electronics' answer to the confusion of the modern battlefield."

The picture shifted to the jet's interior, crowded with computer consoles. Men in olive drab flight suits and headsets hunkered over the displays.

"CCOMS is the most advanced joint-service command, control, communications, and intelligence system in existence," the narrator boasted. "Utilizing its long-range search radar and mobile ground station, CCOMS' wide-area surveillance and target attack system can detect, track, classify, and support the attack of moving and stationary ground targets. With CCOMS, American military units are no longer blinded by what Clausewitz called the 'fog of war'."

Robert Stanning could have used that, I told myself. Not to mention the MPs who died with him.

Now the large screen revealed a combat computer display showing dozens of targets, each one with a special symbol identifying it as friend or foe, aircraft or tank.

"CCOMS' advanced electronics suite includes long-range search radar, high-speed data processing computers, and encrypted communications subsystems, all mounted in a Boeing 707 converted for military use."

The screen now filled with news footage of the carnage wreaked by Coalition aircraft on the columns of retreating Iraqi armor along what the news media nicknamed the "Highway of Death." Burned out tanks, blasted armored cars, and hulks of demolished trucks snaked through the killing field like a serpent of death. Burnt corpses of tank crews hung suspended from hatches, their charred ribs exploded outward by their last breath of fiery air. The camera panned across an Iraqi soldier who made it clear of his exploding tank only to burn to death a few yards away, his legs turned to dust by the intensity of the inferno.

"During Operation Desert Storm, CCOMS cut through the fog of war to help Allied forces turn back the Iraqi aggressors and liberate Kuwait."

The picture returned to the interior of the giant jet.

"Though not yet operational, American military commanders saw the need for CCOMS in the vast expanse of the desert battlefield. Two E-9 CCOMS aircraft and their ground stations were made ready for combat operations. With no air force crews yet trained to use CCOMS, Consolidated Electronics provided volunteer crews to operate the system's intricate electronics. While military pilots flew the big jets and military commanders made the actual combat decisions, civilian employees of ConEl manned and maintained CCOMS' complicated electronics for 49 consecutive days and nights of combat operations, providing our military forces with round-the-clock, real-time surveillance and targeting."

Now the screen showed one of the big jets landing at a desert airfield. As its crew disembarked, air force officers greeted them with handshakes and backslaps.

"Air force officials assessed CCOMS' performance during Operation Desert Storm as excellent and credited the ConEl system with making a significant contribution to the war effort."

The video ended with a fluttering American flag and martial music. The lights came up and the wall slid back to conceal the TV.

"That's our baby," Brooks said. "Pretty impressive, eh?"

My mind still focused on the scenes from the Highway of Death. My last assignment for the news service I used to work for was to cover the Gulf War, or Operation Desert Storm, and I had seen the destruction on the Highway of Death up close and personal. Before the Gulf, I had seen war in a hundred little hamlets and villages in Central America. I carried scars, both physical and mental, from those conflicts. Never, however, had I seen death meted out in such wholesale quantities as I saw in that desert. It added new dimensions to the nightmares that haunted my sleep.

"Very," I finally answered. "In fact, that part about your workers volunteering was very impressive. But I understand you lost one of them?"

Brooks' smile disappeared, his lips closing down on his pearly teeth like an unexpected closing curtain. His head started shaking.

"No," he said. "No, I'm afraid you're mistaken about that."

"Oh, I understood one of your engineers..." I flipped through my notebook as if checking the name. I didn't want Brooks to know how much I knew. "Ah, here it is. Stanning. Robert Stanning. I understood he was killed in some kind of missile attack?"

David Brooks' quick wits failed him. He stared at me, his mouth making little fish-like movements as he tried to think of something to say.

He never got the chance. The door to the conference room opened and four men in business suits walked in. Three of them were laughing at some punch line told before the door opened. The fourth man hustled directly to a wall phone, holding a digital pager in one hand.

"The Commander's Club," Brooks murmured. I don't think he meant me to hear.

Seeing us, the three remaining men suddenly stopped laughing. A stocky man with thinning gray hair and an equally gray, close-cropped moustache spoke first.

"We're sorry, David," he said. A tiny American flag on his lapel glittered from the overhead lights. "We didn't know the room was occupied."

"No, no, major. It's quite all right. We just finished."

I swore I detected a sense of relief in Brooks' voice.

Brooks stood, buttoned, and adjusted his coat. "Gentlemen, this is Mr. Peter Brandt. He's a writer with *San Diego Life* magazine. He's doing a story on how we're coping with the defense cuts. Peter, this is Major Daniel Maxwell, U.S. Army retired." I shook hands with the gray-haired man with the lapel flag.

"Call me Max," he said.

"Call him Mad Max," said one of the other two men.

"Mad Max?" I asked.

"A nickname they gave me when I led an infantry company in Nam," Maxwell said.

Brooks waved to the other two men. "And this Commander Robert Massie, U.S. Navy retired, and Lt. Colonel William Conner, U.S. Air Force, retired."

Massie was the youngest of the four, probably no older than his early fifties. His hair was short and full and still dark, his face clean-shaven. He, too, wore an American flag in his lapel. Conner was the oldest of the men. His thinned white hair had the texture of spider webs. His skin was pale and striated by pink veins. His lapel sported a flag as well. A fifth man entered. He was younger than the rest; I guessed in his late forties. Yet he was completely bald at the crown of his head, and the hair left around his ears and neck was cropped so close his head appeared completely bare. His densely forested eyebrows made up for his naked pate. Beneath the bushy brow were eyes so dark they seemed to possess no pupils. An American flag flew on his lapel as well.

"Ah, Roger," said Mad Max. "David was just introducing us to Mr. Brandt here."

The bald man shook my hand.

"Brandt?" He eyed the scar running down my face. That look used to bother me, but I'd finally gotten over it. There were so many more people in the world with worse scars, both physical and emotional, and the recent war had created many more.

"Peter Brandt," I said. "I'm a freelance journalist doing a story on the defense cutbacks for *San Diego Life*."

"Ah!" The bald man nodded. "Roger Sherman."

"Colonel Sherman, late of the air force," added Mad Max.

"I was just showing Peter our new promotional video for CCOMS," Brooks said.

"Pretty impressive, eh?" asked Mad Max.

"Very," I answered. "I was just talking to David about your workers who volunteered to fly missions during Desert Storm. I understood one of them, Robert Stanning, was killed?"

All three men suddenly seemed to find something else to look at—the floor, the ceiling. One looked at his watch. Finally, Mad Max broke the silence.

"A terrible thing, what happened to Robert," he said. "But no, he wasn't working for ConEl at the time of his death. Robert had left us quite some time before. Right, gentlemen? Must've been, oh—"

"At least a year," said Conner.

"Yes, at least," said Mad Max.

"We were all very saddened to hear of his death," added Massie.

I looked at Sherman. He just shook his head. The glare from the overhead lights slid across his head like a comet, then slid back.

"I'm afraid I'm the new kid on the block. I've only been here a few months. I never met Mr. Stanning."

"Roger is our plebe," Conner said. They all laughed.

"Well, that's strange," I said. "I was recently down at the federal court doing some research on another story, and I came across a lawsuit filed by his widow against ConEl and the government. The suit said he was still employed here when he died."

Mad Max swallowed hard. The corner of his mouth tugged down.

"Poor Susan," he said. "I know she's very distraught. But I haven't heard of any lawsuit. You might take that up with our legal department. If such a suit exists, I'm sure they would know."

"Mrs. Stanning is very upset because Robert didn't always confide in her," Massie said. "I don't believe they had a very close marriage."

Massie gave me one of those looks that suggested it would be very bad manners to pursue this matter anymore. I hated to disappoint him.

"I think I'll take the major's advice and contact the legal department," I said.

"Gentlemen, I'm afraid I have to leave. My wife's in jail. Again."

The man with the beeper broke the line of conversation. He was stocky with a round face, wire-rim glasses, and thinning gray hair. He snapped the pager back onto his belt and straightened his jacket. The American flag also flew on his lapel, of course.

"Peter Brandt, Captain George Krause, retired navy boat driver," said Mad Max. "George used to command a cruiser."

"Now I just play bail bondsman to my wife." Krause shook my hand.

"Another protest, George?" asked Conner.

"Yes." Krause shook his head slowly, then looked at me. "My wife is very involved with the anti-abortion movement. She's been arrested for picketing an abortion clinic. It's only the fourth time. I'm beginning to know all the jailers by their first names."

"Strange bedfellows, isn't that?" I asked Krause.

"What?"

"Your wife being involved in the anti-abortion movement while you work for a company that makes such potent weapons of war."

Krause stared at me coldly. I felt the eyes of the others peering at me, too.

"I don't know what you mean," Krause said, and turned for the door.

Brooks quickly guided me out of the conference room and down the hall to his office. We sat again in the comfortable padded black leather chairs. I crossed my legs and watched him a moment. He smiled back coolly, but his eyes looked everywhere except at me.

"If I may ask," I said, "what did you mean by the Commander's Club?"

Brooks looked at me blankly.

"I don't know what you're referring to," he said.

"When Mad Max and the others came into the conference room, you muttered Commander's Club."

"Oh, you must have misunderstood me," Brooks said. "I really don't remember what I said." He shrugged and looked at me apologetically.

That was when Jack Sweeney took his nosedive off the roof of the admin building.

I left David Brooks there sweating in his fancy English pinstripes, preparing to cope with the worst nightmare of a corporate PR type—the death of an employee on company time. I rode the elevator down with a group of suits from the ninth floor.

"Poor old Jack," one of them said. "I can't believe he did that."

"I can," said another. "He's been a bit loony ever since his son bought it. You should've heard some of the shit he was saying the other day. Talking like there was some kind of great conspiracy against him or his kid." The suit shook his head. "Crazy, really crazy."

Fire and police vehicles were already screeching to a stop near where a crowd had formed to rubberneck at Sweeney's crumpled corpse. A TV news truck pulled in behind them. I ignored them all and kept walking until I heard someone shout my name.

"That's Peter Brandt, all right. I knew it was you."

Michael Larrs was tall, handsome, and looked some ten years younger than the last time I saw him, which was nearly five years before. I had known him when I worked the city for the news service, before transferring to the Mexico City bureau. Larrs was the kind of reporter that gave scandal sheets a bad name. Facts meant little to him, nor did it mean much to him how he got them.

"My, my, my," Larrs said. "Good old Peter Brandt. Back in the old homestead, eh? Got the story already?"

"What story is that, Larrs?"

"This jumper," Larrs said. "We were heading up the 15 for an interview when we heard on the scanner someone took a nose dive off the ConEl building."

"Not my kind of story anymore, Larrs."

I started to walk away but Larrs walked with me.

"Come on, I know you better than that, Brandt. Were you here when it happened? That's the only way you could have gotten here before us."

"I'm not interested in anyone's suicide, Larrs," I said. The blood pounded in my ears. "I don't do that kind of story anymore."

"Like hell, Brandt." Larrs hotfooted in front of me and back peddled as I kept walking. "You owe me, Brandt. You still owe me."

"What could I possibly owe you for, Larrs?"

"For that stunt you and Richardson played on me. Feeding me that phony story about the mayor being gay and secretly marrying his bodyguard. You remember that little stunt, don't you? Took me years to live that down."

I stopped and gave Larrs the most unpleasant look I could muster. "Don't blame Richardson and me for that, Larrs," I said. "That's what you get for stealing other reporter's notes. Now get out of my way and leave me alone."

Larrs stepped aside. I took two steps, stopped and turned back to him.

"By the way, nice face-tuck, Larrs," I said. "You really have to give me the name of your plastic surgeon."

Then I turned and walked back to my car.

CHAPTER 5

It was late afternoon when I made it home. Home was a small bungalow apartment in San Diego's Ocean Beach that also served as my office. It was small and old, and the jetliners from Lindbergh Field liked to do touch-and-goes on the roof all day long. But it was cheap and near the beach. In the mornings, I could jog along the water and cough up all the tar left from when I smoked. In the afternoons, I could take a break and stroll down to the sand to watch the girls in their bikinis and, for a few minutes, I wouldn't feel so old.

The answering machine blinked at me as I walked through the door. The voice on the tape was unfamiliar, and the caller didn't leave his name. I got the message just the same.

"Mr. Brandt," the caller said. "This is the gentleman you've called twice today. I'm sure you know whom I mean. The sunset from the Mt. Soledad cross ought to be spectacular this afternoon. You shouldn't miss it. I personally like to jog that area around sunset."

The tape went dead.

I grabbed my notebook and my tape recorder and went out to the car. The sun was already low over the horizon. I started the Mustang and burned rubber pulling out. As I raced down Sea World Drive toward the I-5, I tried to recall what I had read about the widow Stanning's lawyer, David Needles, in the university library.

Needles was in his mid-forties, son of a career Marine Corps officer. He had made a name for himself by challenging the government and defense contractors over faulty weapons systems that killed service members. Needles had personal motivation for taking on such cases; his father was posthumously blamed for the slaughter of an entire rifle company of Marines in Vietnam. In fact, the massacre occurred because the Leathernecks' newly issued M-16 rifles jammed due to faulty ammunition. It took Needles twenty-four years to clear his father's name.

Needles' most famous case involved an air force fighter crash that was blamed on pilot error. Hired by the pilot's widow, Needles proved to a jury design flaws in the aircraft's control system caused the crash—flaws both the jet's builder and the air force knew existed.

I made the turn onto I-5 and lead-footed it north to Pacific Beach where I got off and fought the rush hour traffic to Soledad Mountain Road. Once there, I gunned the six-cylinders up the road.

Soledad Mountain Road crawled the heights from lowbrow Pacific Beach to the cliff-dwelling wealth of La Jolla. In the Fifties, Mt. Soledad was just another middle-class housing tract. That was before the opulence of "The Village" in La Jolla began climbing the mountain with bulldozers and earthmovers. Now lavish homes leaned out over the mountain's crest on platform foundations and support stilts, while ersatz chateaus and southern estates adorned its slopes.

The peak of Mt. Soledad bristled with broadcast antennae, satellite dishes, and repeater stations. However, what caught the eye from a distance was the three-story white cross that stood vigil at its summit. The foot of the cross was a favorite visiting place for tourists and lovers, or anyone else who wanted to see the expanse of the city, from its Pacific shores to its mountain foothills, in one uninterrupted panoramic view.

I parked the Mustang and walked to the foot of the cruciform. The sun was just beginning its dip into the sea and the sky glowed with reds and yellows. The placid ocean reflected the glow, punctuating it with the occasional phosphorescence of a whitecap. Lights began flickering on the east. A delicate haze covered the city, growing thicker as I looked north toward the giant metropolis of Los Angeles and its crowded suburbs.

When the pain in my head became too bad, or those times when the screams of my ghosts shattered my sleep too often, I would come to this spot to look out over the ocean and seek solace and a little forgiveness. Then one night I found myself considering taking a short drive off a tall mountain, and I hadn't been back since.

There were half a dozen cars parked at the summit, with more than twice that number of people milling around base of the cross. I stood out away from the others, watching for one of them to take note of me. I waited five minutes, then noticed a jogger running up the summit toward the cross. He wore a blue and red warm up suit stained with sweat. A white sweatband held back a swirl of curly blond hair.

The jogger took the right fork in the drive and circled the summit counter-clockwise. He slowed as he approached the others, then stopped as if admiring the view. Still, I watched his head swivel from one face to another, studying each in turn. After a minute, he started his run again.

When he was within a dozen yards of me, we made eye contact. He slackened his gait, then slowed to a walk. When he was fifty feet from me, I called his name.

"Mr. Needles?" The runner nodded cautiously. "I'm Peter Brandt."

"Not here," he said. "Over there, near the trees."

Needles jogged ahead, as if we were merely strangers nodding casual greetings. I waited a minute, then followed at a slow meander.

Needles waited for me beneath a stand of trees from which we could watch the crowd at the cross, the sunset to the west, and the city lights to the north and east. The lawyer studied my face a moment, then spoke.

"Could I see some identification?"

I handed him a business card. He held up his hands as if I were offering him live plague virus.

"I don't want your card," he said. "Those things can be printed up at any Jiffy Print. I want some real ID, something with your picture."

I took my wallet out and handed him my driver's license and an out-of-date police press pass. He studied them closely, then handed them back.

"Thank you, Mr. Brandt," he said. "I'm sorry but I have to be very cautious."

I offered him my business card again. His response was the same.

"I don't want your business card," he said. "I don't want any record of this meeting." He scanned around the summit like a point man on patrol, then turned back to me. "You have to understand, I've never seen anything like this before. I'm under court orders not to talk about the Stanning case. I'm not even supposed to admit it exists."

"I understand," I said. "The gag order."

Needles' eyes narrowed piercingly. "Just how much do you know about this case, Mr. Brandt?"

"Through round-about channels I received a copy of the complaint you filed. Anonymously." I emphasized the last word. "I went to check the district clerk's office to check the court file, and the file disappeared. The USA's office denies such a suit exists. So does ConEl. It's my understanding there's some kind of gag order."

"Gag order, my ass," Needles said. He looked to one side, then to the other, then at me. "Look, this isn't for the record. This is just background. You don't quote me, got it?"

I raised my hands, palms out. "I haven't even brought out my notebook," I said. "Background only."

"This isn't just a court order," he said. "This case has been classified secret by the government. Twenty-four hours after the complaint was filed and served on the defendants, Washington ordered it classified. I had to sign a nondisclosure agreement just to continue litigating it."

"I've never heard of that before."

"Neither have I," he said. "I filed a request to declassify it, but the Information Security Oversight Office squashed it."

"On what grounds can the government classify a lawsuit?"

Needles snickered. "What else? National security." Needles ran a hand through his sweat-matted hair. "I've done a lot of these cases, Mr. Brandt, and they've always claimed national security in some aspect of the case. But this is the worst I've ever seen it. I can't even let my secretary know I'm meeting you. That's why I wouldn't take your calls. That's the reason for all this cloak-and-dagger stuff."

Needles bent down and grabbed his calves, stretching his legs. When he rose, his voice softened. "I'll be honest," he said. "I have a good idea where you got that copy of the complaint. But that's just between you and me, right?" I nodded. He looked around again, then said, "How can I help you?"

"I need more info on the friendly fire incident," I said. "I could only find one story in the newspaper database that looked like it matched the events in your complaint. And DOD denies that incident took place."

"You got what we know," Needles said, shaking his head. "That's all Susan was told. I don't even know about this news story you read."

I told Needles what I had read, then moved on to my needs.

"ConEl says Stanning left the company a year before he died. What do you know about that?"

Needles bent, scratched at the ground, then straightened, a small stone in his hand. He threw the stone sidearm and watched it disappear down the side of the mountain. Then he took a deep breath, letting it out slowly.

"The Stannings' marriage wasn't one of the closest," Needles said. "Susan knows he got up every morning and went to work. When he talked of work, he talked of ConEl. If he left the company, he never told Susan."

"She never saw his pay checks?"

"Automatic deposits."

"So you're saying Susan Stanning can't prove her husband worked for ConEl when he died."

Sweat flew from Needles hair as he shook his head.

"I'm trying to subpoena Stanning's pay records from ConEl and his tax records," he said. "But they could doctor those. I'm planning to depose some employees who knew him. I might get something from one of them. You might have better luck, though."

"Me?"

Needles took the sweatband from his head and wrung it out. "There's a bar where ConEl workers hang out. It's a strip joint on Kearny Mesa called the Launch Pad. Maybe you could talk to some of them there."

He placed the sweatband back around his curly locks and scratched his nose.

"The Launch Pad?"

"Kind of phallic, isn't it?"

"Any other leads?"

Needles started to shake his head, then reconsidered.

"There's one guy you might talk to," he said. "Someone I plan to depose myself. He's the Marine chopper pilot who fired the missiles. He's stationed just up the coast at Pendleton. But . . . "

Needles rubbed his nose again, then grimaced. "But if you're going to talk to him, you'd better hurry. The Corps is drumming him out as mentally unfit. Once they do that, he'll be destroyed as a credible witness for you and me both."

I took the notebook from my rear pocket and flipped it open to a clean page.

"What's his name?"

"Polmar," Needles said, spelling it out for me. "Captain Paul Polmar."

I stopped scribbling and looked at Needles.

"What is it?" he asked.

I flipped back a few pages in the notebook and read my notes from the library.

"Paul was the name of the guy who called the radio station with story of the MP attacks."

The attorney clucked disdainfully. "Well, now" he said. "Now we know why the Corps is drumming him out, don't we?"

CHAPTER 6

As strip joints go, the Launch Pad was a dive. A neon rocket shaped vaguely like a phallus with a lick of flame beneath it beckoned you into a bar dark enough to blind a bat. That was fine, because the waitresses in hot pants and halter-tops were old enough to have kids in college, and the blonde grinding her groin on stage had more cellulite on her thighs than she had silicon in her breasts. And the beer was flat.

Yet the place was packed.

I had spent a futile day trying to get through to Captain Polmar. I tried the direct route first, finding out his air wing and squadron and their office numbers from the base operator. A gunny sergeant at the squadron office bumped me up to the wing commander. The wing commander sent me to the base public affairs office where the PAO insisted I had to make my request for an interview with Polmar through the commandant's office in Washington. The commandant's PAO, in turn, insisted he had no authority to grant such an interview and sent me, instead, to CHINFO, chief of information for the Navy and Marine Corps.

By the time I stopped making phone calls that afternoon, I had gathered enough military acronyms to fill a pot of alphabet soup—and I still had no interview with Polmar, and no likely chance of one. Whatever can of worms the good captain had opened with his call to the radio station, the Corps was obviously determined to keep it resealed. I turned off my computer, switched on the answering machine and drove out to Kearny Mesa and the dark recesses of the Launch Pad.

Men in white short-sleeve shirts and ties occupied the tables around the stage, and as my eyes adjusted to the dark I could see most still wore their ConEl security badges. Pitchers of pale yellow beer sat atop most of the tables. Cigarette smoke drifted to the ceiling. Waitresses shuffled between the tables, performing delicate balancing acts with large trays of beer teetering on their small hands while they themselves teetered on high heels. On stage, the dancer turned her back to the men and bent low until her heavy breasts nearly touched the floor, and swayed her haunches to the belting of a disco beat from the Seventies.

I leaned against the bar, ordered a draft beer and reached for the cigarettes that were no longer there. I dismissed the idea of buying a pack. The beer came, looking as listless as the expression on the dancer's face. I took it and began moving through the tables, one by one. I laid my card on each one, explaining to the customers I was doing a story on downsizing among defense firms. More pretext. After half an hour, I had as much luck as I had with the Marine Corps. I went back to the bar, ordered another beer and wished I had bought that pack of smokes.

A new dancer came on stage, a redhead shorter and younger than the first with a cuter face glossed over with makeup. She smiled and waved with her fingertips to regulars as they threw dollar bills at her. By the time she danced to her second tune, she was down to just a thong and crumpled dollars littered the stage.

A commotion at the entrance drew my attention from the redhead. A tall blonde stood at the door looking around the darkness, ignoring the noise from two heavyset drunks behind her. The blonde moved deeper into the bar. She was slender, with an athletic build accentuated by her tight-fitting blue jeans and white blouse. Her hair was straight and loose, and cut just below the ear. Her face, deeply tanned, made her eyes stand out all the more. They were the color of blue ice.

As the blonde walked deeper into the bar, I noticed she limped heavily on her right leg. I figured she was a dancer recuperating from an injury. She scanned the room, then the bar. Our eyes met briefly and I felt as if I'd been stabbed by a shiv of ice. She turned and took a seat at the bar two stools away.

The men behind her were still making noises. They were construction types, in worn jeans and heavy work boots and greasy with a workday's sweat. The shorter of the two had long sun-bleached hair tied back in a grimy ponytail. A darker moustache curled around his upper lip as he made obscene kissing sounds at the blonde. His partner was bigger, darker, with a dirty beard, and dark hair matted down by sweat and the band of the hard hat he had worn all day. His attempt to lure the blonde was more refined. He simply grabbed his crotch as if offering her whatever might lie hidden there. As big as the drunks were, the bouncer was bigger. He towered a full head above them both, and had the girth and bearing of an ill-mannered bear. His thick, full beard and bulging arms covered with motorcycle club tattoos added to the menacing effect. He moved between the drunks and gently placed his massive hands on their shoulders. The sots visibly shrunk as the bigger man gave them a gentle but clearly hostile warning. They glared at the blonde as they slinked by and sat at the far end of the bar.

Drunks don't learn lessons well. Not ten minutes went by before the darker of the two bought an extra beer and walked it over to the blonde. I couldn't hear what he said to her, but there was no missing her reply.

"Why don't you take your little pencil dick and get the hell away from me?" she said.

The laughter of the bar patrons didn't sit well with the drunk. He grabbed the dancer's arm and spun her on the stool to face him. That was his second mistake.

As she turned toward the drunk, her right fist slammed into his groin. The drunk bent double, grabbing his crotch, this time out of pain. With her left hand, the blonde pushed the drunk's face hard against the top of the bar. He slid to the floor groaning, the blonde standing over him like a Golden Gloves lightweight.

His friend didn't learn lessons either. Ponytail jumped from his seat and raised his beer bottle by the neck, spilling its contents on the floor. He was either too drunk or too angry to notice. The blonde was busy stuffing her money back into her purse and didn't see him coming. The bouncer did, but he was too far away. I reached out as the sot passed and grabbed his ponytail. He rebounded backward like a wrecking yard dog on a leash.

The bouncer grabbed both drunks by their shirts and half dragged them through the exit. The bartender gave me a clean towel to wipe myself, and a free beer for my trouble. The blonde dancer finished packing her purse, and turned to me.

"Thanks," she said. Her eyes held the warmth of an Arctic night.

She was gone before I could respond. I tossed the towel back to the barman and, chagrined, smiled at him shaking my head. He shrugged and walked away. I went to the men's room to wash up.

The restroom had the smell of old urine and stale beer mixed with disinfectant. The walls were defaced with the kind of graffiti you wouldn't expect written by men who came to watch naked women dance. Rust stains ate away at the porcelain in the sink. Once walking into it, I wasn't sure I'd ever feel clean again.

I was splashing my face with cold water when the door creaked open and someone walked in. I grabbed a handful of sandpaper that passed as paper towels and blotted my face dry. The urinal flushed and someone behind me said, "You're the guy who wanted to know about ConEl, right?"

He was short and thin, with a beer belly just beginning to broach his belt. His sandy hair was thin and greased down. Black horn-rims slipped down the bridge of his nose. He pushed them up with his index finger. Behind the lens, his eyes were red from booze. I remembered him from one of the tables I approached.

"That's right," I said.

"You're some kind of reporter or something." He shoved past me to wash his hands.

"I'm a freelance journalist."

He dried his hands then took the business card I offered him.

"Peter Brandt, huh?" He slipped the card into his shirt pocket. "Well, Mr. Peter Brandt, I can tell you everything about ConEl you'd ever want to know. I worked there for 12 years. Name's Sidney Clipper. I'm a weapons engineer."

"*Worked* there?"

"Yeah, well, I got laid off last year. Me and a few hundred other guys. But I keep in touch with my friends here at the Pad. The ones still working there, you know? I still know everything that's going on there."

"Okay, Sid," I said. "You want to sit and talk?"

"Whoa, not now," Sidney said, shaking his head violently. "My buddies'll have my hide if they knew I was talking to a reporter." He glanced at the door like a nervous rat expecting a cat. "But tomorrow, right here about three. Before the plant lets out. Okay?"

I had serious doubts this little nerd could tell me much about what I needed to know, but I wasn't exactly overwhelmed with inside sources. "Sure, Sid," I said. "Three o'clock, here."

Sid scurried out the door to rejoin his pals. I left a discreet time later. The bouncer put a friendly paw on my shoulder and thanked me as I left, and put a handful of free passes for the Launch Pad in my hand.

"Y'all come back any time, hear?" he growled with a southern drawl. "No cover charge."

"Back tomorrow," I promised.

"Anytime, hear?"

It was dark already and the parking lot was unlit. It took a moment for my eyes to adjust so I could find the Mustang. My ears didn't need any adjusting to hear the string of profanities hurled at the night.

It was the blonde from the bar. She was pounding on the camper of a late model Ford four-wheel-drive pickup and shouting a string of obscenities about men that would have embarrassed the proprietor of a bordello. I noticed her right rear tire was flat.

"What the hell do you want?" she demanded as I approached.

"Your tire's flat," I said. "You need help?"

I moved closer and she recognized me.

"Oh, it's you," she said, her voice lower but her tone just as sharp. "Need help? Damn, right I need help. You got any extra spare tires?"

She walked around the car waving her hand at the wheels. All four tires were flat.

"Those assholes from the bar," she said. "They slashed my stems. I saw them drive away laughing as I came out."

"You're going to need a tow," I said. "I'll go call one for you."

The bouncer made a joke of trying to take one of my free passes before he let me back into the Launch Pad to call a tow. When I came out, the blonde was sitting in the rear door of the camper. She held a Styrofoam cup to lips.

"Fifteen, twenty minutes," I said.

"Thanks."

I glanced at my watch and looked around.

"By the time you get that to a service station, its garage will be closed," I said. "You're going to have to leave it overnight. Can I give you a ride home?"

She gave me a look with those blue eyes that nearly gave me frostbite.

"What are you?" she said. "Some knight in shining armor?"

MARTIN ROY HILL

"Fine," I said, stepping back. "Just trying to help. I don't need to make time with strange women." I walked back toward the Mustang.

"Sure. That why you hang out at a joint like this, huh?"

I turned back. I could hear the blood rush in my ears. "I was here working, lady," I said. "I'm a journalist. I was trying to talk to some of those ConEl people for a story I'm doing." I pulled one of my cards out and flicked it at her. It fluttered short of her and landed on the ground. "They were about as friendly as you. Not that it matters much."

I walked back to the Mustang, shaking my head and wishing I hadn't stopped smoking. When I reached my car, I heard footsteps behind me, then a soft, feminine voice.

"Hey, I'm sorry." She held my card up to what little available light there was. "Mr. Brandt. Peter. I'm sorry. That scum left me in a pissy mood. I'm taking it out on you. Could I take you up on that ride?"

I put the keys back in my pocket. "Sure."

"Join me for some wine?"

She poured a cheap burgundy from a jug in the back of the camper and we sat on the pick-up's rear gate to wait for the tow.

"My name's JoAnne, by the way," she said, offering her hand.

"How'd they know which car was yours?" I asked.

"They pulled in behind me," she said. "They must have seen me getting out."

"You hurt yourself dancing?"

JoAnne looked at me as if I spoke Martian. "I'm sorry?"

"Your leg," I said. "I noticed you limped."

"Oh, no." She rubbed her hand against a finely chiseled nose. "A skiing accident. It's getting better."

"You been dancing here long?"

"Ah, no," she said. "Just started really." She patted her right leg. "Bad timing." She laughed nervously and sipped her wine. "So what kind of story did you say you're doing?"

I gave her the pretext line.

"I just need to get to know some of these guys, get to know how they feel about things," I said. I sipped the cheap wine, then asked, "You know any of these guys well enough to introduce me?"

A car pulled into the parking lot, its headlights bathing us in white light. I noticed tiny creases around her eyes and a line where her smile bent the skin. Her face was beginning to lose a deep tan, the type you get only when you spend a great deal of time outdoors. Her golden hair flickered in the car lights as she shook her head.

"I haven't worked here long enough," she said. She tapped her leg again. "And, of course, this happened."

The tow truck came, and JoAnne arranged to collect her car the next day. She climbed into the Mustang and told me to head out to Point Loma, then directed me out along the point itself, through tree-lined avenues lit by dim amber lights into a cul-de-sac that bordered the submarine base.

"That's it," she said, pointing to a collection of three redwood apartments clustered together. "I've got one in the back overlooking the bay."

"Nice," I said, figuring she either made damn good tips or hooked on the side to afford living there.

"Thanks again." She opened the door. Her eyes didn't throw icicles anymore, but I wouldn't describe them as inviting. "And I'm sorry about how I was earlier."

I shrugged it off. "Maybe I'll see you again," I said. "I'm meeting a guy at the Launch Pad tomorrow to talk about my story. About three o'clock. Will you be working?"

JoAnne thought about it a moment.

"I'll be there," she said.

CHAPTER 7

I hate early morning phone calls.

My years as a police reporter and, later, as a war correspondent, programmed me with a Pavlovian response to the phone's ringing in the early hours. The adrenalin surged, my heart raced, my body jerked itself into action so I could dress quickly and rush out the door, often before my brain was fully engaged to cover some tragic and usually deadly human endeavor.

I tried to calm my breathing and steady my heart as I picked up the phone on the nightstand. The voice at the other end was unfamiliar and the caller refused to identify himself.

"I'm a friend of Paul Polmar," he said. "I'm a squadron mate of his, too."

I squinted at the clock. It was just past six.

"What can I do for you, Mr.—" I let the sentence hang as I searched the bed stand drawer for something to write with.

"You were trying to talk to Paul Polmar, weren't you?" the caller asked. "Captain Paul Polmar?"

"Pol—? Yes. Yes, I am," I said.

"You want to talk about the MP incident over there, don't you?"

"The friendly fire incident, yes," I said. "There's been a lawsuit filed over it."

"I want you to know Paul is one of the best men I ever served with," the caller said. "He's one of the best men I know. He *is* the best chopper pilot I know."

"I'm sure he is," I said. Great, I thought. Wake me up to give me a personal testimonial. "That's why I'd like to talk—"

"You're being stonewalled. The Corps doesn't want Paul to talk about it. They don't want to *admit* it happened."

"Why's that?"

The caller didn't seem to hear me.

"No one is happy about this," he said. "The Corps is supposed to be family. We take care of our own. We never leave our dead behind. But they're treating Paul like shit. He's being screwed."

"How is he being screwed?"

"Pressure is coming down from Washington," he said. "They want him out, disgraced. They're killing his career."

"Why?"

"You need to talk to him about that," the caller said.

"They won't let me near him," I said.

"Paul jogs every morning along the beach in Oceanside. You can catch him there."

"What time?"

"About 0530 hours," he said. Five-thirty. "He'll talk to you there. And ask him about the investigation report. *Make* him tell you about the investigation report."

"What investigation report?" I asked. "The investigation into the attack?"

But the line was already dead.

A second call that morning took my attention away from the Stanning story for the day. It came from the L.A. bureau chief of a newsweekly I worked for as stringer for a hundred bucks a day plus expenses. They were doing a cover story on how members of Congress were kiting checks through the congressional bank, and New York wanted background about San Diego's delegation. There was enough slime there to pull together an easy story. I filed my dispatch, sending it by modem into the magazine's computer, called their news desk to tell them to notify the writer who would pull all the dispatches together, and still had time to jog before meeting Sidney Clipper at the Launch Pad.

The bouncer greeted me as I stood in the dark doorway letting my eyes adjust. "Back for more, huh?"

"Can't keep away," I said, handing him one of the free passes he gave me the night before.

"How'd you make out with that chick?"

"What?"

"The blonde with the flat tires." He grinned like a lecher, revealing crooked teeth stained with tobacco. "Jump her bones yet?"

I gave him the same grin back and winked.

"Looks like she's back for more, friend."

His dark locks bounced as he nodded toward the bar. JoAnne sat on a stool, a beer in her hand, watching me. I scanned the tables, spotting Sidney sitting alone with a half-empty pitcher, his neck craned. On the stage above him, a dancer with enough silicon in her breasts to supply the computer industry with microchips for a year swayed out of step with an Elton John tune. I nodded to JoAnne, took a clean glass from a waitress, and sat at Sidney's table. The beer barely broke a head as I poured.

Sidney's eyes blinked blankly as he focused on me.

"Oh, hi," he said. "It's you."

Even in the dim light, I could see the dark semi-circles behind Sid's glasses and the crimson tint to his eyes. He was well into working off one hangover by working on another.

Sid raised his glass to his lips. The stage lights glinted off a gold wedding band. He nodded toward the stage.

"Isn't she incredible?" he said. "I'm a tit man myself."

"How do you get your wife to let you hang out here?"

Sid's face turned stony. He put his glass down.

"Not married anymore." His voice was as hard as his face. "Bitch ditched me after I got laid off. Took my boy and girl with her, too." His face softened a bit. "Want to see their picture?"

Sid's wallet was on the table before I could respond. He handed me a two-by-three-inch color snapshot of four people, Sid, two plump children, and a wafer-thin woman. The woman's image was scratched down to bare paper.

"Good looking kids."

I handed the photo back. Sid gazed at it fondly.

"Yeah, they are," he said. "Good kids, too."

The night before, I told Sidney and his friends I was researching a story on defense layoffs. I figured to stay on this line of questioning until I could work Robert Stanning in somehow.

"So how long you been laid off now, Sid?"

He opened his wallet and slipped the photo into an empty credit card pouch. He didn't have to search for one;

they were all empty. Sid stared at the dancer and counted on his fingers.

"Eighteen, nineteen months."

"What happened?"

Sid drained his glass and refilled it. He pushed his horn-rims back into place, shrugged, and stared at the dancer again. She squatted in front of Sid, her legs splayed, and rubbed her hands up her inner thighs, across her groin and over the twin mounds of her breasts. She rolled her nipples between her fingers, smiled at Sid, then wet her lips with her tongue.

Sid tapped the table in front of me without taking his eyes from the girl.

"Hey, throw her some money, will ya, man? A couple bucks, for both of us."

I crumpled a couple of dollar bills and tossed them on stage. The dancer rewarded me by running her hand between her legs then sucking her fingers. She blew me a kiss, and moved away.

"So what happened, Sid?"

Sid puffed his cheeks and blew air, then reluctantly turned his attention to me.

"Pentagon cut back on one of our missile contracts," he said. "Five hundred of us went out the door, pink slips in hand." His elbows went on the table and he hung his head a moment. "After I gave those creeps twelve years of my life. Nine months later, that bitch of a wife walked out on me."

A waitress gently placed her hand on my shoulder and leaned down, letting the fabric of her halter fall away to reveal the deep cleavage of her breasts. I ordered another pitcher of beer and never noticed her face.

"I guess ConEl's had a long run of bad luck," I told Sid. "Not only have they been losing contracts, but their executives seem to be dying off."

Sid looked at me, his crimson eyes blank.

"I mean, with the deaths of Jack Sweeney and Robert Stanning," I said. "Did you know them?"

Sidney turned his attention back to the stripper, who was now on all fours, backside to the audience, rolling her buttocks rhythmically to a Rod Stewart song.

"I knew Sweeney," Sid said. "Not really well, but I knew him. He was an all right guy. It hit him real hard when his kid took an Iraqi SAM up the tailpipe during Desert Storm. Air force fighter jockey—Sweeney's kid, I mean."

"What about Robert Stanning?"

Sid shrugged and watched the waitress as she bent deeply at the waist to refresh his drink from our new pitcher of beer. This time I noticed her face. She was the redheaded dancer I watched the night before. I paid her for the beer, plus a healthy tip to her match her attributes.

"I've heard of Stanning," Sid said. "Never met him. He sort of disappeared sometime of go. There were rumors going around he was killed somehow over in Saudi." He shrugged again.

"You ever hear of the Commander's Club, Sid?"

"Sure." Sidney looked at me as if I had asked him what Disneyland was. "They're a bunch of retired military officers, former project officers. You know?"

"No, I don't know."

Sid shifted in his chair and leaned against the table. He quickly looked around him as if he were about to reveal the secret of the Holy Grail.

"They come through the revolving door," he said. "See, in the military it's up or out. If an officer gets passed over for promotion two times, it's Good-bye GI Joe and don't let the doorknob hit you in the skivvies on your way out."

Sid gravely sipped his beer and looked around again.

"You don't earn promotion points being a project officer with a defense firm. No up-and-comer wants that assignment. So the Pentagon assigns all these pass-overs to these project officer billets to wait for their retirement. And if they play along with the company execs, they can have a guaranteed job waiting for them when they retire."

Sid twirled a finger in the air.

"You see? Like a revolving door."

"Is that legal?" I asked. "It's sound like a conflict of interest."

Sid snickered in his beer. He placed the glass down and looked at me like I was hopeless.

"Now it is," he said. "But it used to be SOP. Congress passed a law in the Eighties saying retiring project officers couldn't be hired by the same company they worked with. So what do they do? They just get hired by another division or subsidiary of the same company."

"So there was a loophole built into the law?"

Sid's head bobbed up and down, his mouth set in a sardonic grin.

"Big enough to fly a C-5A through."

I'd already sized up Sidney Clipper and figured his ego was as inflated as the price of beer in this joint. I could use that to my advantage. I leaned across the table, glanced sideways a couple times, and said in a conspiratorial voice:

"Sid, I'm going to take you into my confidence. I think I need your help."

Sid leaned further across the table, the crimson whites of his eyes growing wider. I told him my real story assignment, about the Stanning lawsuit, how Stanning seemed to have disappeared only to end up dead in a blown up armored car on an Iraqi battlefield. When I finished, I looked at Sid gravely.

"I have to admit it, Sid," I said. "I'm stumped. I've slammed up against a wall. I need to know who this guy Stanning was and what he was doing in Iraq. You sound like the man who can help me breach that wall."

Sidney twisted his mouth around and nodded thoughtfully. He took a sip of beer and straightened in his chair.

"You're right," he said. "I can help you. I didn't know this guy Stanning, but I know guys who did. I can ask around, see what I stir up."

The entrance door opened and Sid turned to see who came in. His bravado disappeared as suddenly as it appeared.

"Damn," he said. "I know these guys from ConEl. I can't let them see me talking with you. I'll call you when I've got something."

Sid picked up his glass and the pitcher of beer and scurried to a table on the far side of the stage. Three men in short-sleeve dress shirts sporting ConEl security badges joined him. Sid was suddenly animated, gesturing with his arms, his cupped hands forming huge breasts in front of him.

"Was that your—" JoAnne stood at the table, watching Sidney Clipper make more obscene gestures. "What do you call them? Snitches? Informants?"

"How about adolescent?"

"Certainly seems to fit." JoAnne flashed a smile full of straight white teeth. "But what do you really call them?"

"Sources," I said. "Can you sit?"

"Sure."

The red-haired waitress came by and took my order for two more drafts. JoAnne grimaced as she sat in the chair Sid had left, and adjusted it so she could keep her right leg straight.

"Leg getting better?"

"Slowly but surely, the docs tell me," she said. "Too slowly and not too surely for me, though."

"Everything work out with your truck?"

"Oh, sure," JoAnne said. "Four new tires and two hundred bucks poorer. Thanks again for your help last night."

"De nada."

The waitress came with our beers and a disapproving look for JoAnne. I handed her a ten, and she gave me back enough change to tip the dancer once.

"What's this?" I asked, tossing a two-buck tip on her tray. "No employee discount?"

The waitress took her tip, smiled tightly at me, and patted my shoulder.

"Not unless you're offering me one of those brews, honey," she said before gliding away with her hips swaying.

JoAnne dismissed the remark with a tilt of her head.

"Jealous little bitch, isn't she?"

I just raised my eyebrows and sipped my beer.

"So what kind of story did you say you were working on?"

I told her the pretext story again. However, something told she might be more helpful if she knew the truth.

"I lied," I said. "The story's really about a lawsuit that's been filed against ConEl by a woman whose husband used to work there." I told her what I told Sidney, then told her she could be helpful if she took note of any conversations among ConEl workers that might seem to have some bearing on the fate of Robert Stanning.

JoAnne thought about what I said, and shrugged again. "Sure," she said.

I gave her one of my business cards, then we sat in awkward silence while she studied it intently. I watched her face in the glow from the stage. Even in the dimness, her eyes seemed incandescent. They radiated a cool confidence I didn't think any man could ever shake. She flashed them once at me, then turned back to the card. I felt a cold sweat break along my spine and a strange mixture of both fear and arousal. I wondered what she would be like to know better. For a brief moment, I thought I would try. Then rational thinking kicked in and I knew every man who saw those eyes, that face, or watched her dance on that stage had the same thought. I shook myself from my reverie, pushed my chair back from the table and stood.

"It's been good meeting you, JoAnne," I said, offering my hand. "Even if we got off to a rocky start. I hope I hear from you."

She shook my hand with a firm grip. Her eyes bore into me and I felt that same strange mixture of emotion again.

"I'm sure you will," she said.

I drove home by surface streets, taking the long, straight drive along Balboa Avenue toward Pacific Beach and Mission Bay. The sky above the ocean was vibrant with yellows, reds and oranges as the sun settled behind the thin line of the horizon. I stayed on Balboa as it turned into Garnet Avenue and followed it through Pacific Beach to the Crystal Pier. I had nowhere to go now, and talking to JoAnne had left a deep, vacant aching in my chest that I needed to exorcise.

Traffic was unusually light near the beach and parking was ample. Still, I chose a spot a block from the pier and used the distance to stretch my legs. A faded blue and white arcade stretched across the entrance to pier, welcoming all to Crystal Pier. I walked through the gate and past the tiny blue and white bungalows that rented out by the day or week. The pier swayed gently as waves rolled through its pilings. A gull danced in eddies of wind sweeping around its frame. The end of the pier widened and I leaned against the chipped and scarred wood of its railing breathing deeply the smell of brine, bait, and fish scales. The sun finished its performance and slipped away. The lights of the city flickered on. The air turned cold. I began to shiver and walked back to my car, the aching still in my chest.

I drove back up Garnet to Ingraham and rode over the bridges crossing Mission Bay. Lights from the bridges danced on the water like strange, misshapen angels. I took SeaWorld Drive into Ocean Beach and parked my car in the driveway outside my bungalow. Normally I would have jumped out, locked the car, and hurried into my home. But the same pair of headlights had been behind me since I drove down Balboa, and they were with me again as I drove across Mission Bay. I sat in the Mustang, the lights out, and watched in the rearview mirror as a dark sedan slowly prowled the street.

Five minutes passed and the car hadn't returned. I went up to my front door, and fumbled with my keys in the dark. I needn't have bothered. The door swung open at my first touch. I froze. The bungalow was dark and quiet. I reached inside and flicked on the light.

I'm not much of a housekeeper, but it was obvious someone was a worse visitor. Sofa cushions were tossed on the floor. Desk drawers were opened and their contents spilled on the floor; the same with the papers in the four-drawer metal file cabinet. The computer was switched on, its screen glowing blankly.

A window slid open in the bedroom. I rushed back outside and saw the dark figure of a man running past my car and out to the street. An engine started out of view, and a white van with dark side windows and its lights out roared into the street to meet the intruder. They were gone by the time I made it curb side.

CHAPTER 8

I shot awake bathed in sweat, my heart racing, my lungs gulping for air, looked around the dark bedroom, and reminded myself it was just a dream.

Just a dream. A nightmare really. A nightmare I couldn't wake myself from just a few years before, because it wasn't just a dream then. It was real. Each night I relived it in my head, it seemed more terrifying than before: the roar of the storm-swollen river, the riveting staccato of Morgan's Mac-10, the look of surprise on Frank's face as the small bullet entered his forehead, Herman's last scream before he died. Then there was Matt, the old bear of a man, laid out in the street, torn and bleeding, by a car bomb.

I reached into the nightstand drawer for the half-empty pack of cigarettes I left there for the nights the dreams became too bad. The first lungful of stale tobacco smoke made me gag, the second went down easier. Then I remembered the break-in.

Probably the break-in triggered the nightmare. It was obvious the intruder wasn't there to steal valuables. I don't own much in that way to begin with, but what I did own—a portable Japanese color TV, an old stereo set, a VCR I acquired from my dead ex-wife's estate—had been left untouched. The thief was after something in my files. I pretty much guessed what that was, and I knew he hadn't found it.

I'd worked too long in countries where search warrants were written on the heel of a boot to leave my notes and documents lying around. After chasing the intruder, I returned to the bungalow, took a letter opener from the desk, crossed the room, and pried a four-socket electric plug from the wall. It was a fake outlet, and behind it was hidden enough space to conceal the Stanning suit and my typed notes with enough room left to hide a small ransom of jewellery, as if I had such a thing. I checked the papers to see if they were still in the order I'd left them, then put them back in the wall and replaced outlet facade.

It took the rest of the evening to get my place back in order. Afterward I had a couple of drinks and some dinner, then slept in fits through the night until I woke in that cold sweat with enough adrenalin rushing through my veins to wake all the dead in Arlington National Cemetery.

§

My head was beginning to ache, the old wound throbbing in rhythm to my heartbeat. I put the cigarette out and padded into the bathroom for my painkillers. The toilet was hissing loudly. It'd been running all night, adding sound effects to my dreams. I jiggled the handle, then went to the kitchen to make coffee. It was still hissing when I came back to run water into the washbasin for a shave. I jiggled the handle again before stepping into the shower, but it was still running when I stepped out to dry off.

I lifted the tank lid to see if the drain plug was blocked. It was.

Crammed into the tank was a brick-sized package wrapped in aluminum foil and a plastic bag. I didn't need to lift it out and open the bag to know its contents. I'd seen enough kilo bricks of stash to recognize one on sight. From its smell, it was probably high grade Thai.

I didn't need to think about it much. I knew who had put it there and I knew why. I wrapped the brick in a towel, put the lid back on the toilet and flushed it several times. I took the towel and the brick into the bedroom and dropped them into my rucksack along with a 20-pound weight from the weight-lifting set I pretended to use. Then I pulled on my jogging shorts and Saucony running shoes, swung the rucksack over my shoulders and ran as fast as I could toward the beach.

I was never a strong runner, not even in high school when I didn't smoke or drink, and had youth on my side. But with the hemp in my bag, I could have competed in the Olympics. The muscles in my shoulders ached with the strain from the shoulder straps. My legs pumped like pistons, while my arms hammered the air with each step. My lungs burned.

Small homes and apartments flashed by in a blur of color. I studied each car as I approached it, waiting for its doors to swing open, its occupants to jump out and yell, guns in their hands. But each parked car was empty, and each that rolled past simply kept on rolling.

I made it to the beach and turned south on the esplanade. The sky was gray with a morning marine layer and the brine-tinged wind off the ocean was cool, yet sweat rolled down my side and streaked my chest. My breathing was coming harder now, each breath a clumsy gasp. The wound in my head pounded like bass drum. I sped past other joggers as if I was doing the 440, dodged between elderly walkers, and narrowly avoided colliding with a young couple holding hands while rollerblading.

Just ahead was a public restroom. I weaved between three more skaters, darted into the men's room then smashed into a wall of flesh and soiled rags.

"Hey, man, watch what the motherfuck you're doing!"

He must have been six-five, but he couldn't have weighed more than one-seventy. His blue jeans were torn and faded, but it wasn't a fashion statement. His red T-shirt was brown with sweat and grime. He wore a tattered jungle field jacket with torn epaulets, a ripped out cargo pocket and coloring so faded the camouflage pattern blended into one vague primary hue. A filthy beard covered his face, and long, tangled hair of indeterminable color fell across his shoulders. The stench of body odor was indescribable.

"Who you think you are, pushing me around like that?"

The bum's dry, cracked lips parted to bare teeth so rotted they looked canine.

Dark malevolent eyes stared out from the rat's nest of his face. He carried a bedroll under one arm and a plastic bag full of soft drink cans beneath the other.

"Sorry, man," I said, backing away from the smell.

"Okay," he said. "Hey, can you spare some change for coffee or something?"

I held my arms out to my sides. "Sorry, I never carry money when I run."

The bum sneered and pointed a filthy finger at me. "Well, you just watch where you're going from now on," he said. Turning, he mumbled: "It's not safe for anyone to walk around here no more."

I waited a half minute to make sure he was gone, then whipped the rucksack off my shoulders, pulled out the towel-wrapped brick and shoved it deep into the trash can. I flushed the urinal for effect, shrugged the rucksack back on and jogged another hundred yards down the esplanade. Gulping for air and holding my head, I watched the surf rolling up the beach and got an idea. I peeled off my running shoes and socks, stepped off onto the sand and ran into the ocean. I let the rucksack drop onto the sand where the surf would flush it out, then swam several yards back and forth parallel to the shore. When I finished, I picked up the pack and its weight, rinsed off in a public shower, then jogged slowly back to the bungalow.

They were waiting for me when I arrived.

They waited until I entered, then I heard someone shout, "Police! We've got a search warrant!" A booted foot kicked the back of my knees and sent me face first into the rug. A rush of heavy boots trampled past me. A knee went to the small of my back and my arms were yanked around and cuffed. A cold, thick gun barrel was stuck behind my ear.

"Don't move, fucker!"

I didn't move.

A German shepherd brushed past me, sniffed my face, then the rucksack at my side, and moved on. A hand gripped my left elbow and yanked me to my feet. There were at least six men in my house, all in plain clothes but wearing blue police raid jackets. Two stood watch over me while the others ransacked the bungalow, spilling drawers on the floor, toppling furniture, tossing folders from the file cabinet. One led the K-9 from room to room on a leash.

"Narcotic Street Squad?" I asked.

"You guessed it, scum sucker," said the narc holding my arm. He wore his hair over his ears, and had a goatee beard.

"Get the wrong street address again?"

Goatee told me to shut up, but I saw the other cop watching me check the address on the warrant then pop outside to check the house number. He came back in, a satisfied smile curling a black moustache flecked with gray.

"Peter Brandt?"

"That's me. Who are you?"

Goatee shoved me down onto the sofa. The cushions were gone, and the steel suspension springs cut into my legs and buttocks. The pain in my head sent flashing lights stabbing through my ocular nerve.

"Lt. Holden. Where have you been, Mr. Brandt?"

"Jogging."

"What's in the backpack?" Holden picked up my bag and looked inside. Deep crevices lined his face, and his black hair was thinning badly on top. His eyes were dark and expressionless. He removed the 20-pound weight and held it out to me. "What's this?"

"A weight," I said. "It makes the workout harder."

"Why is this bag all wet?"

"I dropped it on the shore when I went for a swim," I said. "The tide was higher than I thought."

Holden dropped the weight back in the bag, then let the bag drop carelessly to the floor. It landed with thud that made Holden's men jump. Holden looked at me with his dead eyes, his moustache twisting down.

"We got a tip you're storing drugs."

"Who gave you the tip?"

"Don't be funny."

"I'm not," I said. "Someone just called you up and said I've got drugs here and you just wake up a judge to get a warrant and storm my place? Cops don't work that way. You know that. I know that."

Goatee gave me strong shake. "What makes you think you know how cops work, asshole?"

"I'm a journalist," I said. "I used to be a police reporter for a daily newspaper."

Holden and Goatee looked at each other. Holden's' eyes remained empty, but Goatee's eyes turned up as he sighed.

"Great."

"Who do you work for?" Holden asked.

"I'm a freelance now," I said. Then I named the newsweekly I string for to impress Holden. It didn't seem to.

"You spend a lot of time south of the border, don't you, Brandt?" he demanded.

"I used to work for a wire service out of Mexico City," I said. "I traveled all around the region."

"Including Columbia?"

I nodded.

"Ever meet anyone from the drug cartels?"

"I talk to people," I said. "That's my job. I've met with drug smugglers and DEA agents."

"And what about Palm Springs?"

I didn't answer. I thought I saw a glint in Holden's eyes. I knew he didn't get this stuff from any street stoolie.

"Didn't you get in a little trouble in Palm Springs a couple years back? Something to do with drugs and pornography?"

"Someone killed my ex-wife and my best friend," I said. "All I did was figure out who did it." I returned the lieutenant's hard stare as best as a half-naked man in handcuffs could. "You seem to know an awful lot about me, lieutenant. Considering you said you just got a tip."

Holden didn't answer. He gave Goatee a look and Goatee shoved me against the sofa's backrest.

Find anything?" Holden shouted to his men.

"Nothing, lieutenant."

"What about the dog?"

The dog's long tongue swirled wetly around its lips as he led his handler from the kitchen.

"Nothing, skipper," the handler said. "Nothing except a steak thawing in the reefer." The handler grinned at the shepherd. "Brute thought it was delicious."

Brute trotted through the living room, savoring his snack. He sniffed me casually as he passed. My breathing stopped as the dog turned to the rucksack again. Brute, however, merely gave it another cursory sniff, then trotted out the door, his tail wagging.

Holden, however, wasn't quite as happy with the results of the search. His moustache twisted down in a deep grimace and his nostrils flared. He nodded to his men, and they beat a hasty retreat out the door. The detective lieutenant nodded to Goatee, who stood me up to unlock the cuffs, then shoved me back onto the sofa. I felt the springs dig into my spine. My head felt like it split in two. I placed my palms against my temple and tried to push the pieces back together.

"Sorry to have troubled you, Mr. Brandt." There was little sincerity in Holden's voice.

"Yeah, sorry, scumbag," Goatee said, hooking the cuffs through his belt.

"That's it?" I squeezed the words through the pain. "No 'May we help you clean up this mess?'."

Holden reached into his shirt pocket, took out a business card and flicked it at me.

"Hire a service. Charge it to the city," he said.

Then he left.

CHAPTER 9

The next morning I woke early, pulled on my running clothes and drove north to Oceanside to look for Captain Polmar. I had spent the rest of the previous day once again straightening up my little bungalow and nursing my headache. The latter won out eventually and I downed more painkillers and went to bed, the day a loss.

The morning marine layer cast a gray pall over the shoreline. I found a place to park and jogged slowly along the beach. It would be easy to spot the Marine officer. Seagulls and sandpipers owned the beach, their squawks and shrieks rising above the chorus of the waves. The morning's surfers were all off shore, straddling their boards and rolling in the swells waiting for the next big one. Only a few surf anglers and beachcombers otherwise intruded on the birds' domain.

My steps and my breathing merged into a rhythm, and my mind began wandering through the events of the past few days. I was hesitant about the Stanning story when Tom Collier gave me the assignment. Editors habitually hype story ideas when they commission them, especially if they had a personal stake in the assignment. Collier obviously had just that and it was more than just doing a favor for an old flame. Since the Stanning file disappeared from the court clerk's office, however, I started thinking there might actually be a story there. Now I was certain of it.

Obviously I had touched a sore spot somewhere, but where and how eluded me. The kilo brick and the narc squad's raid were meant to get me out of the way. Whoever planted the Thai stick also tipped off Holden, and whomever that was had to have some pull with the cops. Under normal circumstances, the SOP for the narcs would be to put me under surveillance and move in only when they were certain to find me with drugs. But Holden had moved instantly on the tip, and he knew more about me than he could possibly have uncovered in such a short time. That meant whoever decided I was too much of a nuisance had a lot more authority than Lt. Holden did.

I ran and walked the beach for an hour. The sun was burning off the marine layer and the beach was filling with more joggers. The birds retreated to a sandy knoll near a short breakwater. I gave up on Captain Polmar and walked back to my car. The parking spots were filling up, but one car stood out—a dark brown sedan, a Chrysler. A man wearing dark glasses and a light blue sun hat sat behind the wheel reading the morning paper. He ignored me as I toweled off and fired up the Mustang. Still, as I pulled away from the curb, the brown Chrysler pulled out, too. He stayed just a few cars behind me all the way back to Ocean Beach.

§

The phone was ringing when I stepped from the shower.

"Yeah, uh, Pete? Sid Clipper here, from the Launch Pad?"

Clipper's voice was thick and uncertain. "Like I, uh, told you, I talked to some buddies last night. Think I found some things out about this guy Stanning."

The desk drawer creaked as I opened it and fished for a notebook and pen. I dropped into the chair and cleared a space on the desk to write.

"Yeah, Sid. So what do you have?"

Sidney's answer had to wait until he'd finished a bout of hacking. "Ah, yeah, Pete," he said. "Think you could come out to my place? I'm not feeling too good this morning, and what I got to say I think would be easier to explain in person."

I took down Sidney's address and hung up just as he was consumed by another coughing fit. The brown sedan was behind me again as I headed east on the I-8 toward Tierrasanta. He stayed a cautious two car lengths behind me, but in the rearview mirror, I could easily make out a splotch of the blue hat through his windshield. I wasn't willing to let him stay there all the way to Sidney's. I got off the interstate at Hotel Circle, and nosed the Mustang into the eternal traffic jam known as Mission Valley.

They say all roads lead to Rome. With Mission Valley's chaotic tangle of roadways that might be true, because none of them seemed to lead anywhere in the continental United States. From the Hotel Circle off ramp, I nosed the Mustang east on the frontage road past the Valley's restaurants and hotels. I made the crossover to the north side of the freeway, twisted through two or three turn-abouts, and sped along the frontage road until I reached one of the valley's two big shopping malls. The Mustang's six-cylinder roared and its tires squealed as I bumped over the driveway into the center's parking lot. The sedan stuck with me as I sped around the lot until I came to the double-deck parking structure and gunned through it. A battered station wagon suddenly backed from its space, looming before me like an ancient dreadnought. The Mustang swerved once to the left, then to the right, its radials screeching, and sped clear of the giant.

Blue Hat wasn't so lucky. His brakes shrieked like the death screech of a giant bird. The crunch of metal and tinkling glass echoed through the concrete structure. I weaved slowly back through the aisles to view the scene. The Chrysler had struck the corner of the old station wagon. It was like a speedboat hitting a battleship. The Chrysler's front end looked like a wad of used foil. One head light hung suspended by its wires, the other lay in pieces on the ground. The station wagon looked no more battered than before.

The wagon's black driver was as ancient as his automobile. He waved his arms and hurled curses at Blue Hat, who paid him no attention. His focus was on me as I idled past. Even through the dark glasses, I could feel his glare.

§

The apartment complex where Sidney Clipper lived sat at the bottom of a bluff in Tierrasanta, a relatively new residential area built on what had once been a WWII artillery range. Live shells were still found among the homes and apartments. Unfortunately, sometimes children found them. One thing I'd learned about war was its horrible legacy lived on long after the fighting stopped. In Vietnam, Central America, Kuwait and Iraq, and even here, children were still paying the price for the stupidity of their fathers and grandfathers.

Despite the new construction surrounding it, Clipper's apartment complex looked like it had once been a target for artillery practice. It was a two-story stucco shoebox, with no covered parking, no pool, and no greenery. The brown stucco was pocked, and its tan trimming chipped and pealing. Sidney's apartment was nothing more than a cubicle, a bootlegged room carved from the two-bedroom unit next door.

"Not much, huh?" Sidney said, letting me through the sliding glass door that served as his only entrance.

Sidney's unkempt bed took up most of the space. A portable TV, toaster oven and hot plate, and a tiny refrigerator filled the rest. The kitchen sink was also the washbasin for the attached bathroom. The only other room was a closet.

"I used to live in a three-bedroom ranch house," Sidney said. "Now look."

He sat on the bed and lay back, holding his head. His voice was still thick. His eyes were their normal crimson, but the shadows beneath them were much deeper.

"So what do you think of Chateau Clipper?" he said.

Two cheap watercolor seascapes that must have come with the apartment hung on the walls, one above the bed, the other above the TV. The remaining walls were covered with centerfolds, the kind where nothing is left to the imagination. The only other wall decorations were a dartboard near the refrigerator and a decoupage wall hanging that looked like the insides of a computer.

"I've lived in worse," I said, exaggerating only slightly. I pointed to the decoupage hanging. "What's this, Sid?"

Sidney seemed to forget his hangover. He sat up, his face lightening and his lips twisting into a crooked grin. "That, my friend, Peter, is the guidance system from a cruise missile," he said proudly. "I smuggled the parts out from the plant piece by piece."

"That doesn't sound like a very smart thing to do," I said. "What would ConEl do if you got caught?"

"Oh, hell, Pete." Sidney waved my concern away. "Everyone in the industry does it. I know a guy in L.A. who's got the guidance system from a MX missile displayed in his living room."

"Doesn't the government miss these things?"

Sidney snorted and shook his head.

"They can't keep track of anything," he said. "That's why the industry's able to charge them up the butt hole for everything. Half of everything your tax dollar pays for ends up in someone's front room or den. Hey! I've forgotten my manners."

Sidney stood up quickly, and regretted it. He sank back onto the bed, shaking his head and blinking his eyes, before trying again more slowly.

"I've forgotten my manners," he repeated, his voice weaker. "I don't get much company. Would you like a cup of coffee?"

"Sure."

He shambled to the sink, filled a pan with water, and placed it on the hot plate.

"All I've got is instant," Sidney said. "Hope that's okay."

I told him it was fine, and followed his steps to what passed as the kitchen. Tacked to the dartboard was a newspaper photo of Thomas Hess. The tiny holes pocked the pictures, and two plastic-finned darts stabbed the CEO's forehead.

"Anyway, like I said, the government never keeps track of anything." Sidney washed two plastic coffee cups as he talked. "There was this guy—boy, did he have a scam. He ran the etching department, where they make the negatives for acid etching microcircuitry."

"Etching microcircuitry?"

"Oh, yeah," Sidney said. "What they do is make a photographic negative of the circuitry design and use that to chemically etch the design into the circuit boards. Like the way printers make plates for their presses. You know how that works, right?"

I did, and told him so.

"Same thing."

He dried the cups with a paper towel and placed them next to the hot plate. The pan on the burner began to hiss and steam.

"Anyway, we're supposed to run the used developer through a recycling machine to recover the silver nitrate for the government. See, they pay for the developer, so they want the recovered silver. But, like I said, no one really pays any attention. So this guy starts filching the recovered silver. He had a baggy locked in his desk filled with silver dust. Must've been worth a small fortune!"

Sidney's laughter stopped only when he saw I didn't appreciate the theft of my tax dollars.

"Yeah, well, that's the kind of stuff that goes on, you know." He looked at the dartboard and snickered. "That guy there, Tom Hess, he's the biggest sneak thief of all."

Sidney dried his hands, then pulled a dart from Hess's forehead.

"They lay me and a few thousand other guys off to save money, then this guy gives himself three million bucks," he said. "That's your tax money, too, you know."

The dart flew from Sidney's hand and landed in the wall. Sidney pulled it free and hammered it into Hess'ss nose.

"That reminds me," he said. "The asshole's coming into town tomorrow for Jack Sweeney's memorial service at the plant."

The refrigerator door creaked as Sidney opened it and stooped to look inside. He took a jar out and opened it.

"Uh-oh. Need a new jar of coffee."

Sidney opened the closet door and reached to the top shelf, which he used as a larder. The tiny closet was only half filled with clothes—a couple of suits, several short-sleeve white dress shirts, and a few trousers. A small cache of firearms filled the rest of the closet. Sidney turned with a new jar of coffee and followed my eyes to his gun collection.

"You like guns, Pete?"

"Not particularly," I said.

Shrugging, Sidney closed the closet and made our coffee. It was instant coffee at its best, bitter and tasting like anything but real coffee.

"So, Sid," I said, growing impatient. "What about Stanning?"

"Oh, yeah, yeah."

Sitting on the bed, Sidney closed his eyes and tried to remember why he had called me there in the first place. He removed his glasses and rubbed his eyes. Without the magnification of the lenses, his eyes looked rat-like. Their crimson whites only added to the effect.

"Jesus, these guys are paranoid now," he said. "You'd think you were asking them to spy for the Commies."

"Paranoid? How so?"

"Yeah," he said, slipping the horn-rims back on. "I guess the Pentagon sent down a new security liaison officer. Some army captain named Joe Rice or something like that. They call him 'Cold As Ice' Rice."

Sidney looked at me and waited for me to comment. I sipped my coffee and waited for him to continue.

"Right, Stanning," he said. "Seems your boy Stanning was involved in some kind of black project. Something called Quarry."

Setting the coffee down on the sink, I pulled out my notebook and flipped to a fresh page.

"You said Quarry?" Sidney nodded and I scribbled the word. "What do you mean 'black project, Sid?"

"You know, an off-the-books project."

"No, I don't know, Sid. What's that mean?"

Sidney suddenly sat straight on the bed and adjusted his glasses.

"Well, Mr. Reporter," he said. "I probably shouldn't be telling you this "

Shouldn't but you can't resist, I thought.

"But the defense industry does a lot more than just build missiles and guns, my friend. Sometimes the government asks us to go above and beyond, you know what I mean?"

The frown on my face told Sidney I didn't.

"You ever hear of CCOMS?" he asked. I nodded. "Did you know that during Desert Storm, CCOMS went operational with a crew of ConEl technicians because the Air Force didn't have any trained crews?"

"Yes, I did, Sid," I said. I finished the ersatz coffee and put the cup back on the sink. "I saw the promotional film ConEl put together about that. Are you trying to tell me that was some kind of covert operation?"

"No, that was overt," he said, his lips puckering into a pout. "Sometimes they're overt, sometime covert. ConEl once sent me to Israel to work on their missile program there. Had a fake passport and everything, just like James Bond. That was covert, and all done at the request of Uncle Sam."

I began to think I'd underestimated Sidney's Walter Mitty complex.

"Sid, why would the U.S. government send you to Israel undercover to work on their missile program?"

"Plausible deniability, my friend." Sidney eyed me suspiciously, his ego deflated.. "Uncle Sam didn't want the ragheads to know we were helping Tel Aviv develop a short-range ballistic missile to carry their nuclear warheads. That's why."

"And Stanning?"

Sidney lay back on the bed, removed his glasses, and rubbed his eyes again.

"I don't know what he was working on and neither did my friends."

"Thanks, Sid."

I flipped the notebook closed and pocketed the pen. Sidney's raised hand stopped me short of leaving.

"Hey, Brandt, that's why it's called a black project. No one's supposed to know about it."

He sat back up and slipped the horn-rims over his nose again. His voice was tense, earnest, the thickness from his hangover almost gone.

"I'll tell you one thing, Brandt," he said. "That crap about Stanning leaving the company a year or so before he was killed? It's just that, crap. He was on ConEl's payroll up to the day he bought it."

"How do you know that, Sid?"

"Because he never left, Pete," he answered. "Couple of the guys I talked to last night have offices on the same floor as Stanning. In fact, in the same hallway. He had an office there until he took off for wherever he went before they found him in Raghead Land."

"They're sure of this?"

Sidney nodded confidently.

"In fact, the day ConEl got word Stanning was dead, they immediately cleaned out his office. The way my friends described it, the guys cleaning it out acted like they were sanitizing the place."

"Who cleaned it out?" I asked.

"ConEl security."

"Whose orders?"

Sidney shrugged.

"Would ConEl's payroll records show he still worked for them at the time he was killed?" I asked.

"I doubt it," Sidney said. "One thing about black projects, Brandt. You got to have black funds to run them. That's probably how he was paid."

I stared at Sidney a long time, chewing over what he had said. His bloodshot eyes began to flutter and close. He lay back down and wrapped an arm over his head.

"Oh, man, I don't feel so good suddenly," he said. "Must've been the coffee."

I slapped Sid on the leg and thanked him.

"You done real good, Sid," I told him. "You're an ace operative."

"Hey, Brandt?" Sidney's voice thickened again. "Go out to the plant tomorrow and watch the ceremonies. Watch Hess come to town. He puts on quite a show."

§

By the time I got off the I-8 in Ocean Beach, I was certain I was being tailed again. It was a different sedan, a red Pontiac, and I could see no hint of the blue hat above the steering wheel. But the car had been behind me since I left Sidney's, and it stayed with me as I cruised the surface streets back to the beach. At a stoplight, the driver of the sedan had no choice but to pull close to me. As he did, I noted his license plate number and scribbled it in my notebook.

I figured the only way anyone could still be following me after I lost the first tail was if they were running a tag team, a multi-car surveillance with two-way radios. My first hunch was the Narcotic Street Squad, but I dismissed that right away. The first shadow showed up before the Thai was planted in my toilet. The narcs wouldn't have been tipped off until whoever called them was certain the contraband had been planted.

No, I had to go back to my original conclusion. Whoever had tipped off the narcs had authority that far exceeded Lt. Holden's. And that meant the feds. But which? FBI? DEA?

I knew someone who might be able to help me find the answer not only as to who was tailing me, but also to what Robert Stanning and Project Quarry were all about. If feds were following me, they probably also had my phone tapped. Fred Danbury wouldn't be happy with me at all if I called him on a phone I thought was bugged.

When I reached the bungalow, I rushed in and grabbed a handful of coins from a jar I kept in the kitchen. My pocket loaded and jingling, I walked down to the beach to where I knew there was a pay phone, dropped a few dollars' worth of coins into the slot, and dialed the number of a travel agency in Orange County to the north.

CHAPTER 10

S idney Clipper was right. Thomas Hess did put on a
big show. From the way David Brooks kept
nervously eyeing me, it was obvious ConEl's flak
was not happy about my seeing it. I could understand
why.

It wasn't Sidney, however, who convinced me to see
the event. It was something JoAnne, the dancer, told me.
Her voice was waiting on my message machine when I
returned from calling Fred Danbury. She wanted to meet
me at the Launch Pad at five. After bantering with the
bouncer, who started calling me his best regular, I found
JoAnne seated in a booth at the back of the club. She
wore a powder blue T-shirt tucked with military precision
into her tight denim jeans. She was leaning back against
the wall, her bad leg propped on the seat of the booth.

She waited until a waitress brought us a couple of
beers. Then, wincing as she lifted her leg off the seat, she
turned to face me and propped her elbows on the table. In
the darkness, her azure eyes seemed to glow with a light
of their own.

"I overheard some ConEl guys talking last night," she said. "They were talking about this Stanning guy you're interested in. I couldn't hear everything, but one guy said someone named Sweeney knew too much about him— Stanning, that is. Does that mean anything to you?"

I thought about it and shrugged.

"Maybe," I said. "Did they say what this Sweeney knew?"

JoAnne's hair moved like waves as she shook her head.

"That's all I could hear," she said. "With the music and everything. Do you know this Sweeney?"

Her eyes bore into mine like a laser.

"He was an executive at ConEl," I said.

"Was?"

"He died a few days ago. He killed himself by jumping off the roof of the ConEl admin building."

JoAnne's eyes flashed when I mentioned Sweeney's suicide but it didn't last long. Her eyes refocused and cut deeper into mine.

"Why did he do that?" she asked. "Do you know?"

"I understand he was despondent over his son's death," I said. "He was killed in Desert Storm."

"That's sad." As she said it, I wondered if JoAnne's eyes ever showed compassion. "Did you know him?"

I shook my head. "I was there at ConEl when he died, sitting in the flak's office as he went off the roof. It didn't make the flak's day, that's for sure."

I finished my beer and excused myself, dropping a ten on the table for her trouble. It was dark as I left the bar, and I sat in the Mustang in the unlit parking lot mulling over what JoAnne told me. I decided then to attend Hess's arrival, hoping to use the occasion to find out more about what Jack Sweeney knew about Robert Stanning.

Something else gnawed at the back of my mind. JoAnne had been so inquisitive—too inquisitive, in fact. I tried to put it off to the same Walter Mittyism that drove Sidney Clipper to want to help me. That was a logical conclusion, but as I started the Mustang and put it in gear, I had the uneasy sensation I was just interrogated. Now, watching the arrival ceremonies, I was about to understand why.

The entire company was made to turn out on the athletic field to watch the spectacle. A dais worthy of a presidential inauguration was built at one end of the field. American flags flew at half-staff at either end of the stage, and a third was draped behind the lectern. The lectern's polished veneer glistened in the sun. A red carpet extended from the stage stairs through the crowd of workers, ending perfectly at the curb where an honor guard of ConEl security guards stood in formation decked out in stiffly starched dress uniforms, glinting boots laced up to their knees and peaked caps.

As a special guest of David Brooks, I sat in the reviewing stand reserved for corporate execs and VIP visitors. Brooks sat four seats away with the mayor, his hair stiff and unresponsive to the wind whistling through the bleachers. He seemed uncomfortable with the mayor, and he constantly glanced my way as if he hoped I'd get bored and go home before Hess made his entrance. I was almost sorry to disappoint him.

Hess arrived from the airport in the lead limousine of a five-car motorcade. Tiny American flags whipped violently at the end of each front fender of his limo. An escort of six motorcycle rent-a-cops led the procession through the gate to the reviewing area, sirens wailing. The honor guard snapped to attention, their boots clicking in unison. Then the man who had wrecked so many lives stepped from the limousine onto the red carpet. Thomas Hess was short for such an industrial giant. He couldn't have been more than five-six, and probably wore lifts to reach that. In his sixties, his hair was iron gray turning to white. His skin was too tan for a man who spent his life in a boardroom, reminding me I read an article saying the government accused Hess of buying a yacht with Pentagon dollars.

Hess stood at the edge of the carpet, hands crossed and surveyed the crowd of workers with empty eyes. Only when the athletic field echoed with their applause did he proceed forward, walking slowly toward the stage with one hand held limply in a regal wave. The honor guard followed at a discreet distance.

The GT CEO mounted the stage as if he were about to be coronated, but I got the impression simple coronation would not have been enough for him. Standing at the lectern surrounded by Old Glory and the guards was a man whose corporation had driven good people to acts of corruption, whose leadership had driven his own companies into the ground and rained pink slips on his workers like a New York ticker tape parade, a man others endowed with the power of life and death for communities as well as companies.

As the echoes of applause died out, Hess adjusted the lectern microphone and began his eulogy of Jack Sweeney. Even with the amplification of giant speakers, his voice was thin and reedy.

"Brutus began his eulogy of the great Roman emperor by saying, 'I come to bury Caesar, not to praise him.' Well, I come here today to praise Jack Sweeney, an honorable man, a man who gave his all for his country both in peace and in war."

I watched the crowd of workers, wondering how many would remain employed when the man at the lectern finished his corporate eulogy for ConEl.

"Jack Sweeney knew the need for a strong America," Hess's tinny voice continued, "and he personally knew the sacrifices some of us must make to keep America strong. Only a few tragic months ago, Jack's son paid that ultimate sacrifice when his Air Force fighter jet was shot down by an Iraqi missile . . ."

Some of the workers dabbed their eyes. I wondered if they cried for Jack Sweeney or for ConEl. Hess droned on and, as I listened, I wondered if his speechwriters suffered from delusional paranoia.

"Like Jack, we all must make sacrifices. In today's New World Order, some of us must sacrifice our jobs, our paychecks, perhaps even our homes, to ensure that General Technologies remains strong. However, we must remember that by doing so, we will ensure America remains strong. I'm certain Jack Sweeney would agree . . ."

Hess's self-righteousness would have made my blood heat to boiling if I hadn't seen something else that turned it to steam faster. Standing at the corner of the bleachers, partly obscured by the spectators, was an army captain who looked more than familiar.

I worked my way down the viewing stand, never taking my eyes from her. Her blonde hair was pinned beneath a black beret. In place of the jeans and T-shirt she wore last night were Class A dress pants and tunic, both starched and GI-creased. Crossed flintlock pistols were pinned to her lapels indicating her specialty as a military police officer.

She didn't spot me until I was almost on her, turning toward me as if my stare was like a tap on the shoulder. Her azure eyes showed only the slightest surprise, then became hard and cold.

The black name badge on her dress blouse read RICE. I remembered what Sidney Clipper had told me about ConEl's new security liaison, *Cold As Ice Rice*. Only the Joe was spelled without an E, short for JoAnne.

"So is stripping just a way to supplement your captain's salary, or is there something kinkier to it?"

My voice had the hard edge of a saber, but her eyes countered with a cold that would have shattered tempered steel. I understood how she got her nickname.

"I never told you I was a stripper, Mr. Brandt," she said, her voice as cool as her stare. "You made that assumption yourself. I simply didn't disabuse you of it."

Hoping to melt her ice, I turned up the heat. "Listen to me carefully, captain," I said. "It's against the law for the military to spy on private citizens, and if you have any doubt about that let me disabuse you of it right now. Get your goddamn tail off me now. If you don't, or if you try to frame me with any more planted contraband, I swear I'll hit you with an ACLU lawsuit so damn fast it'll make your captain bars crack."

It worked. For just a moment, her eyes lost their frosty stare. It was enough for me. Before another blizzard could set it, I turned and started back for my seat. Her hand on my shoulder stopped me.

"We've got to talk," she said. The ice in her eyes had melted.

"I can't see what else we have to talk about, captain." I kept my voice sharpened to an edge. I started to turn, but her reply stopped me.

"To begin with, I don't have anyone following you," she said. "And I'd like to know why they are."

"Why?"

"Because I'm investigating the death of Robert Stanning, too."

It seemed I stared at her long enough for the entire viewing crowd to take notice of us, but her words had actually only registered in my hearing when they were followed by the crack of a rifle shot and the angry whine of a high-powered slug screaming toward its target. On the dais, one of the security guards fell back against the flag-draped wall, his head disintegrating into a bloody pulp splattered against Old Glory.

Thomas Hess, the man whose empire built the biggest and deadliest weapons in the world, stood frozen in terror at the carnage created by a single, cheap, low-tech bullet. The screams of the crowd and the sudden pounding of their feet drowned out the second shot as they stampeded for safety. It found its home in Hess's left shoulder, striking on the angle and powdering a large chunk of his shoulder blade against the Stars and Stripes. Hess did a half pirouette, then a guard threw himself over the CEO and took him to the ground. The third shot struck the guard in the neck as he sheltered Hess.

Jo's instincts were the same as mine. We hunkered behind the limited safety of a lamppost, afraid more of the panicking crowd than of the shots fired at the stage. VIPs in the grandstand were no less hysterical than the workers in the athletic field. A woman was sent tumbling down the stairs by a shove from a well-heeled man who thought she moved too slowly. Jo and I pulled her unconscious body from the path of the stampede before the panicked VIPs trampled her to death.

The firing stopped. The athletic field echoed only with the screams of panicked workers and visitors, and the cries of the wounded and injured. I followed Jo to the dais, fighting the torrent of flesh desperate to flee the killing zone the stage had become. A few of the security guards had the presence of mind to form a perimeter around the platform, their drawn pistols waving futilely in the air as they eyed the field for any sign of the shooter.

On the stage, the American flag cried crimson tears. Blood pooled and spread from the three men lying there. The platform was slippery with it. Those still on the stage moved as if stricken by catatonia. A man whose skin had turned ghost white stood at the lectern, his suit splattered with blood and bits of human flesh and brains, his eyes wide and unseeing as he droned endlessly into the microphone: "Please do not panic. Please do not panic. Please . . ."

Thomas Hess lay on his back to the right of the lectern, unconscious. Someone pressed a handkerchief against the CEO's left shoulder. The makeshift dressing quickly turned red, while a pool of darker blood grew wider from beneath the chief executive. I leaned down and turned Hess over.

"You need to apply a pressure dressing to the exit wound in his back," I told the man with the handkerchief. "That's where he's bleeding out."

The man stared at me as if I'd told him I was from Mars. His face was the color of newly fallen snow and his eyes were vacant. Like the man at the lectern, he was deeply in shock himself, and I wondered how they both were still upright. I turned to Jo.

"Do you have any sanitary napkins in your purse?"

Now it was Jo's turn to stare at me.

"What?"

"Sanitary napkins," I repeated, my voice sharp and rising. "They make good dressings. Do you have any in your purse?"

"I-I guess so." She dug around in her black GI purse, then pulled out two panty liners and held them out to me. "Here."

I grabbed the packages and ripped them open. They were too small to do much good, but they were all I had. Then I looked up, saw the flag on the backboard, took a small penknife from my pocket, and ripped a swatch from Old Glory. Hess's skin was cold to the touch as I pressed the flag-wrapped panty liners into his wound. The compress turned warm from the blood it absorbed. The hand of the man with the handkerchief was as cold as Hess's skin when I pressed it against the second dressing and told him to keep pressure against it. He nodded silently and did as told.

I stepped over Hess and looked at the two prone security guards. The first one hit was beyond help. Everything he was or ever thought was now splattered against the dais. The second guard was alive but probably not for long. He lay on his back, while one of the surviving guards pressed a handkerchief to his neck to staunch the blood.

"God damn it, we need help here," cried the guard, whose nametag read BROWNE. "Harry can't breathe. It sounds like he's drowning. Where are the damn paramedics?"

Leaning over the wounded guard, I listened to his breathing. It was strained and shallow. A gurgle accompanied each difficult breath.

"He *is* drowning," I said.

Taking a ballpoint pen from my shirt pocket, I pulled the tip and its attached ink reservoir out with my teeth, then did the same with butt cap. Then I straddled the injured guard and put my little knife to his throat.

"What the hell you doing?" screamed Browne. "Get the hell away!"

Browne tried to push me away but I was balanced better than he was. I pushed back hard, and he tumbled onto his ass. Ripping off the handkerchief dressing, I felt along the wounded man's trachea until I found the notch at the bottom of his throat. Browne rose up again, but Jo stopped him short with a shove.

Another guard, older and grayer, came over and grabbed him.

"It's all right," he told Browne. "I seen them do this in Nam."

I slipped the tiny knife blade into the notch, missing bone and cartilage and slicing through muscle until I hit the windpipe. The tube from the ballpoint pen slipped easily into the incision, and as it did, the injured guard took a deep spastic breath. A funny whistle came from the tube in his throat as his breathing became deeper, steadier.

Placing the kerchief back against the wound, I nodded to Browne to take over. He moved into place without looking at me. As I stood, he muttered a simple thanks, but never looked at me again.

The screams of panic died out. The athletic field was empty save for those injured by the stampede. The wind carried their cries along with the wail of distant sirens. Jo took my arm as I stood looking at the chaos wreaked by the shooter.

"I've got to go," she said. "They think they found where the sniper was." The ice was gone from her eyes, replaced by an earnestness that nearly bordered on pleading. "Meet me at my place tonight at seven. I really think we need to talk."

I nodded dumbly and watched her run across the athletic field toward the main gate.

§

A caravan of black-and-whites, fire trucks, and ambulances careened through the main gate, their sirens screaming. Fighting my way against a human tide of police officers, fire fighters and paramedics, I reached the parking lot just as the first of the press arrived. A white TV van abruptly braked next to me and Michael Larrs jumped out.

"Jesus Christ, Brandt," he said, looking me up and down. "Are you hurt?"

I looked down and realized for the first time blood covered my clothing. I shook my head and tried to wipe some of the bloody grime from my hands, suddenly shamed by my appearance. A cameraman came up behind Larrs, handed him a microphone, and pointed his videocam at me. That snapped me out of my stupor.

"Get your god damn camera off me, Larrs," I growled, walking away, "before I cram it up your ass."

Larrs followed me, his lens jockey right behind him.

"So, Brandt, tell us what happened here," Larrs said, tipping the mike at me. "You saw it happen, didn't you?"

"I didn't see a thing, Larrs."

"Come on, Brandt. Tell us what happened. How'd you get blood all over yourself?"

Turning abruptly, I snatched the microphone from Larrs' hand and stepped close enough to him to see the makeup-caked pores on his face.

"First I'm going to cram this up your ass," I told him, sticking the mike in his face. "Then I'm going to cram the camera up there." I pointed to the cameraman. "And after that, I'm going to cram him up there. So, unless you want to get real personal with your lens jockey, Larrs, back off."

The muscles in Larrs' face tensed. His eyes flickered between each of mine. His lips twisted, then relaxed, and he waved the cameraman away.

"Fine," he said, as I turned and walked toward my car. "But I'd really like to know how coincidental it is that Peter Brandt was here at ConEl both times someone gets killed? You're working on something. What?"

Larrs followed me to the Mustang, never pausing in his harangue.

"You're going to tell me, or I'm going to find out. I swear that, Brandt."

I backed the Mustang abruptly, just missing Larrs by inches. I tried harder after putting it in first, but the newsman bounded out of my path. I left him behind, screaming curses at me and at the world in general.

CHAPTER 11

One long, hot shower, two stiff drinks and a couple of smokes from my nightmare stash of cigarettes later, I was feeling almost like I could forget the events of what happened at ConEl. But I knew that was a lie. Like Macbeth's wife, I would be trying in vain for the rest of my life to wash from my memory the blood of that day.

I pulled a casual sports jacket over my khaki shirt and jeans, and kept the window open on the drive out to Point Loma. I hoped the brisk night air would blow away my ghosts. It didn't. But it did clear my head enough to let me remember the way to Jo's apartment and arrive there five minutes early.

Jo's apartment was one of two perched above garages in a small, six-unit complex. The apartments were divided between two buildings trimmed in redwood, with Jo's walk-up and her neighbor's sitting at the end of a long driveway bordered by an ivy-covered fence. The flat itself had all the warmth and hominess of an empty aircraft hangar. Though not large, the starkness of the front room made it seem cavernous. The only furniture was a sofa and matching hassock, and a typewriter table in the corner that held a laptop computer. A potted fern sat opposite the computer, its leaves brown and drooping. There was no TV, no stereo system. A boom box sat on a windowsill playing a Jackson Brown tape, the volume turned low. The bare hardwood floor and the naked walls made the music sound louder than it was.

The counters in the adjoining kitchen were as barren as the living room was austere, and I suspected the cupboards and the refrigerator were just as empty. Yet I felt strangely comfortable with the apartment's Spartanism. It was the home of someone used to living out of shipping crates and suitcases, and to me it felt familiar.

The huge bay window made up for what warmth the furnishings lacked. From it, you could look out over the entrance to San Diego Bay and watch the tiny red and green navigation lights of passing ships twinkle like stars against the black universe of the darkened channel. Across the channel were the runway lights of the North Island Naval Air Station and beyond that, across the bay, rose the jagged skyline of downtown San Diego. The landing lights of jetliners approaching Lindbergh Field looked like falling stars dropping amid the skyscrapers. Farther south, the Coronado Bridge flickered with the headlights of cars and trucks crossing the bay. On a clear day, you could probably see the lights of Tijuana.

Jo waved to a small dinette where the living room and kitchen merged.

"Sorry, I don't cook much," she said. A smile of chagrin played at her lips. She pointed to a tiny table cluttered with two place settings, several cartons of

Chinese takeout, and two bottles of wine. "As you can probably guess, I entertain even less."

Her hair was loose. It glistened and moved easily as she turned. She wore pale pink sweats and white Reebok running shoes, and it struck me that I'd never seen Jo wearing a dress or a skirt.

"I wasn't expecting dinner," I said.

"Well, I figured I owe you that much," Jo answered. "You haven't eaten, have you?"

I shook my head.

"Good." She picked up the two wine bottles. "I wasn't sure what kind to serve with Chinese. Red or white?"

I shrugged. "Either, I guess."

She chose the red, and opened it like a master. Pouring two glasses, she offered me one, then drank the other in almost one gulp. She smiled self-consciously and dabbed at her lips with her finger.

"I told myself I wasn't going to have a drink until you got here," she said. "After what happened today, I really needed it."

"You had more discipline than I did," I confessed. I emptied half the glass and Jo refilled it.

Jo waved me to a chair and started dishing out fried rice, kung pao chicken, and sweet and sour pork. She finished, and sipped her wine, looking at me. Her blue eyes seemed dimmer, the light within them gone.

"Well, you deserved a few drinks for what you did today," she said. "You probably saved both their lives."

"How's the guard doing?" I said between mouthfuls.

"He lost a lot of blood, but he'll be okay," Jo said. She chewed on some rice then answered the question she had expected me to ask. "Hess is in serious condition, but he's expected to pull through."

"I wasn't really interested in the pompous asshole, frankly," I said.

"I don't blame you," Jo said. For the first time I could remember, she really smiled. It was wide, friendly, and crooked and reminded me of a tomboy's smile. "I wasn't interested when I was told either."

We laughed over that, a little harder than it deserved, the wine beginning to warm our thoughts. The light started to flicker again in Jo's azure eyes.

"Where'd you learn to do that? What you did to the guard?" Jo asked.

"I used to report for a wire service," I told her. "I did a lot of reporting from Central America, covering the fighting in Nicaragua, Salvador, some of the crap that was going on in Honduras that officially wasn't supposed to be going on. I took some first aid training, you know, just to be prepared."

"You learned that in a first aid course?"

"No." I chewed on some peanuts and chicken and shook my head. "There was an older guy in Salvador who'd covered Vietnam, Angola, the Falklands. He learned to do it in Nam after watching a GI drown in his own blood after being hit in the throat just like that guard. He just couldn't forget that and taught everyone he ever went into the field with how to do a tracheotomy just in case he ever needed someone to do it to him."

"Well, if you ever see your friend again," Jo said, "I think that guard would like you to extend his thanks."

"I'll never see him again," I said. "He's dead, killed by a landmine in Nicaragua."

Jo gazed at me with a look of embarrassment. "He didn't die because there was no one to do a—what did you call it? A tracheotomy?"

I stared at Jo a long time, chewing on my food and my thoughts. My first instinct was to change the subject. Then I figured, hey, she's a big girl. She wears an army uniform. So I told her.

"There was nothing left to do a tracheotomy on," I said. "It was what they call a Bouncing Betsy. It doesn't go off until you take your foot off the pressure plate, then it shoots an explosive charge up into the air." I made a cutting motion at chest level. "It took off everything from here up."

I shoveled more food into my mouth and chewed while Jo stared at me in silence. Then she emptied the red wine into our glasses and opened the bottle of white. She took a deep breath and let it out slowly.

"Well, I guess Chinese goes with both red and white," she said. After a minute she asked, "Did you cover Desert Storm?"

"As much as the military would let us," I said. "We were pretty restricted on where we could go, or what we could see, or whom we could talk to."

"I understood it was all over television," Jo said. "That doesn't sound very restrictive."

I stopped eating, set down my fork, and thought carefully about what I was going to say next.

"For the most part it was just a bunch of guys standing in front of military hardware repeating what was said at briefings," I said. "For instance, some of us heard rumors that the Patriot missiles weren't as successful at destroying SCUDs as we were being told. We were never allowed to visit the areas being impacted by SCUDs or to view SCUD debris at the locations where they were supposedly shot down."

"And?"

"Israel was relying on American Patriot batteries to protect its population from Iraqi attacks. That was part of its agreement to stay out of the war. Well, we were told— and the TV jockeys were reporting—that the Patriot missiles had an eighty to ninety percent interception success rate. The latest information today is that the intercept rate was probably as low as ten percent. Israel was so disgusted by the bad performance of the Patriot missiles, they started planning their own attack on Iraq. If that happened, it could have started World War III. If we had been able to report the truth about the missiles' failure, it could have averted an Israeli attack. Fortunately, the ceasefire was signed before Israel could attack."

Jo was quiet for moment, then said, "Hmm," and drank some more wine. I decided to change the subject.

"What about the shooter?"

"He must've been on the roof of a building across the street," she said, beginning to eat again. "They think they found the place, but it was clean. He didn't even leave his brass behind. We could've gotten prints off it if he had."

"Any suspects, motive?" I felt a strange sense of *deja vu* as I lapsed into what had been a standard line of questioning when I worked as a police reporter.

Jo leaned back and laughed, and nearly choked on a mouthful of rice.

"Only a few thousand disaffected workers Hess has laid off," she said, struggling for composure. "Not to mention dozens of business acquaintances the old fart has screwed with over the years." She washed down the rice with a sip of wine. "The man is more disliked in this country than Saddam Hussein."

We ate in silence for a few minutes, the conversation used up. I stared out the window a bit, pretending to watch the ships in the channel but actually watching Jo's reflection in the glass while she watched me. Finally, she caught me watching her and smiled with embarrassment. I did, too.

"So " I stopped and thought a moment. "What do I call you? Captain? JoAnne?"

"Jo is fine."

"So tell me, Jo, how long have you been in the army?"

She counted the years in her mind. "Seven years next month." She lifted the glass to her lips and added in a half mutter: "If I make it that long." She finished her sip, then shook her head when I waited for her to explain. "Nothing."

"What made you join?"

"I was an army brat," she answered. "Dad was career army, retired a general. You might have heard of him, Clayton Rice?" I indicated I hadn't. "He was a big hero in Korea. He won a couple Silver Stars."

I raised my eyebrows to show I was impressed with her old man's credentials. "So you followed in his footsteps?"

Jo smirked. "Dad wanted his *boys* to follow in his footsteps," she said. "Dad was always disappointed his youngest child was a girl. I was supposed to be named Joseph, after a friend of his who was killed in Nam in the early years."

"And when you were born he settled for JoAnne?"

"Not quite," Jo said. "He wanted to name me Josephine. Thank God mom stopped him!"

Our laughter was honest but short-lived. Jo's eyes sparkled for a moment, but quickly dimmed again.

"Rob, my oldest brother, was going to carry on the grand tradition. He went to West Point. Graduated near the top of his class. Went to jump school, then qualified with the Rangers before shipping out to Nam. He was killed there."

I told her I was sorry and I meant it. I knew the pain never went away.

"My older brother was killed at Hue with the Marines," I said.

Jo's lips pursed as she looked at me before slowly lowering them to the table.

"Well, dad would have been prouder of Rob if he'd died like your brother." Her voice was tight and disdainful. When she looked at me again, her eyes glistened with tears.

"Rob was murdered by a VC whore who..." She stopped to breathe deeply. "Who slashed his penis and left him to bleed to death in an alley." Her head inched side to side, then she looked at me with eyes that looked as if they had never held life. "Dad . . . never forgave Rob for that."

We each picked at the food on our plates as we let silence shroud us. Only after we each emptied our glasses and Jo refilled them did she break the quiet.

"Anyway," she said. "My youngest brother, Marcus, was expected to follow Rob to the Point. He had the grades, and he was a great athlete. But he . . ." Jo smiled and groped for the words. "But he didn't have the right sexual preferences, if you know what I mean."

"He's gay?"

"And dad never forgave Marcus, either," she said, nodding. "Not even when Marc was dying from AIDS."

"Your father doesn't sound like a very forgiving man," I said.

"He wasn't," Jo said. She stared into the darkness beyond the window. "I always felt I was dad's final disappointment. Being a girl, you know? So after college, I joined up. Went to OCS, got my commission. I thought maybe I could make his dream come true. Thought maybe he'd . . ."

Jo shook her head and sipped her wine.

"But dad never approved of women in the military. Thought they were a waste of taxpayers' money. He died about six months before I shipped out for Desert Storm." Chagrin played with her lips again. "At the time, I thought that was the cruelest joke ever played on me. There I was going to war where I could finally prove myself to dad, and the old fart was dead."

Jo stifled a sob, while I suppressed my own instinct to reach out and touch her. There was none of the hardness in her face I saw at the Launch Pad. Gone was the icy coldness in her eyes that had given Jo her nickname. She looked vulnerable, like a small girl lost and alone. But she would not let herself be that way for long. In a moment, the toughness returned to her face and her eyes drew frosty with some distant memory. Then she seemed to remember where she was and smiled her crooked smile.

"Didn't matter much though," she said. "I never got to prove myself anyway. I was sitting in a transit barracks in Saudi when it got hit by a SCUD missile." Jo rubbed her injured leg at the memory. "Now I'm just waiting to hear if the army's going to let me stay in or if they're going to drum me out with a medical discharge."

"What happens if they do?"

Jo shrugged. Her straw colored hair fanned around her face as she shook her head. "I've sent resumes to some security firms," she said. "But . . ."

She took a sip of wine and shrugged again. Then she smiled at me and changed the subject.

"Enough about me, Mr. Reporter," she said. "What about you?"

"What about me?"

"Well, let's begin with that scar over your right eye," she said. "That must've been pretty nasty. How'd you get it?"

Like a reflex, I reached up and touched the scar. It wasn't as bad as it was before, and I'd stopped wearing dark glasses to hide it. But I was still self-conscious as hell about it.

"Pretty ugly, huh?" I said. I hated the apologetic embarrassment I heard in my voice.

"It doesn't detract too much from your natural good looks, if that's what you mean," she said. "I was just curious. Bar fight? Or did you just ask the wrong question in an interview?"

"Took the wrong picture," I told her. "A couple Salvadoran soldiers didn't like it and they smashed my camera with their rifle butts. Then they tried the same thing with my head."

Jo's eyes studied the blemish with a new interest.

"Does it still hurt?"

"Sometimes," I said. "Mostly it just causes me headaches."

I shrugged as if it didn't matter and tried changing the subject.

"Anything else you'd like to know?" I asked. "Or was that it?"

Jo thought a moment, then pried some more. She would have made a good reporter.

"Married?"

I shook my head.

"Divorced?"

All I did was nod, but she saw something else in my face.

"Oh, oh," she said. "I know that look."

"What look?"

"The divorced-but-still-in-love-with-her look," Jo said with a certain smugness. "Every single woman knows it and hates it."

"Don't worry about it. She's dead," I said, a little too sharply.

Jo's smugness vanished. Her mouth trembled slightly as she tripped over her apology.

"I'm sorry. What happened?"

I just didn't feel like advertising my own miserable failure with personal relationships, so I didn't tell Jo my wife left me because I felt my career was more important than hers. And I didn't want to explain how Robin was murdered because I wasn't there to protect her the way I promised her I would. And I wasn't going to brag how I hunted down her killers at the cost of my best friend's life, among others.

"She died," was all I said. The look on her face said Jo realized she had stumbled into an emotional minefield. Like a smart soldier, she backed out of it.

"I'm sorry, Peter," she said, after a sigh. "I guess I've never been good at small talk."

"Me neither," I said. "Maybe we should just get down to business?"

"Maybe we should," she agreed.

CHAPTER 12

T hat's all you know?"
I told Jo what I knew about Robert Stanning how he was found in an Iraqi hospital, how he was killed in the friendly fire incident, his widow's lawsuit, the disappearing court records, the office Stanning kept at ConEl and how it was sanitized after his death. Her tone of voice indicated she didn't believe me.

She was right. I hadn't told her about Project Quarry, the black project Sidney Clipper said Stanning was working on. I wanted to keep one ace in my boot in case I needed it later.

"I've only been working on it less than a week," I said. "And I must have turned something over or I wouldn't be under surveillance and the narcs wouldn't have rousted me. I just don't know what it is."

I was sitting on the sofa in the living room sipping coffee Jo had made. She made it better than Sidney Clipper did. While we talked, Jo paced the hardwood floor as best as her bad leg would let her. Her short blonde hair rolled in waves as she shook her head.

"It's still next to nothing," she muttered.

"Isn't it time you start sharing with me what you know about Stanning, captain?"

Jo stopped and turned toward me, her eyes spiked with frost. I could feel the chill run down my spine and all the way to my toes. Then she sighed, the eyes warmed a bit, and she relaxed. Her lips pursed and she nodded.

"The Pentagon wasn't too concerned at first when Stanning was found in that Iraqi hospital."

Jo sat across from me on the hassock, hands clasped.

"But after the fighting stopped and our intel units started going through captured documents, they began to get worried."

Jo looked around for her coffee cup, found it sitting on the rim of the planter, and took a sip. "You know anything about Iraq's unconventional weapons program?" she asked.

"Hussein was trying to build the bomb," I said, nodding.

"He was trying to build several nuclear bombs—warheads, actually," Jo corrected. "And the ballistic missile systems to deliver them. What our intel units found was that Hussein had acquired a great deal of advanced American missile technology. That's when they started worrying."

"From what I've read in the papers, it seems half the country was selling Saddam U.S. technology with the encouragement of the White House."

Jo shook her head, sending her blonde hair a-twirl.

"Not this kind of missile technology," she said. "This was our most advanced stuff. With this technology, if Hussein had enough oil money and the wherewithal, he could have built a missile capable of delivering a nuclear warhead to Washington, DC. Fortunately, Saddam had neither the money nor the wherewithal. Nevertheless, the fact he was able to get his hands on this technology has a lot of people in Washington worried."

"What's this got to do with Stanning?"

"That's what I was sent here to find out," Jo said. "We believe a lot of the technology Hussein got came from West German companies he was doing business with. Many of those companies are also subcontractors on some of our missile programs. Stanning emigrated to the U.S. from West Germany, and became a naturalized citizen. He held dual citizenship. You know he used to work for ConEl, but left or is supposed to have left the company to freelance as a consultant. Apparently, he was acting as a liaison for several German and U.S. companies doing business with Baghdad.

"After the embargo was ordered on Hussein, we believe Stanning sneaked into Iraq to deliver more missile technology to Baghdad. Some of that technology we now know came from ConEl's files. What I need to find out is if Stanning stole that technology to sell it, or if he was acting as a conduit or maybe even an employee of ConEl."

Jo stood and stretched her bad leg. She limped across the floor, one arm crossed against her chest propping the other. The cup in her hand hovering near her lips, but she was too deep in thought to drink.

"I went to the Launch Pad that night we met for the same reason you did—to talk to some employees, see what I could find out." She smiled her crooked grin at me. "I guess I figured I'd use my womanly charms to seduce them into talking to me. Unfortunately, it worked on the wrong two Neanderthals." Jo paced the floor some more, then continued.

"Anyway, that little altercation blew my chance to talk to anyone," she said. "Then when you helped me with my flat tires and told me you were a reporter doing a story on ConEl—well, I figured I'd just play along, see what I could find out from you."

She sat on the edge of the couch and touched my leg. A jolt of electricity jumped through me.

"I'm sorry about that, Peter," Jo said. "I didn't know what else to do."

I echoed her apology. "I shouldn't have assumed you were a stripper," I said.

"Actually, I found it kind of flattering in a way," Jo said, showing her crooked grin.

She suddenly inhaled sharply and let it go, stood and limped across the room sipping her coffee.

"So, let's cut to the chase, Jo," I said. "What do you know about the mysterious Robert Stanning?"

Jo stopped pacing and lowered her cup. "About as much as you, I'm afraid," she said. She sighed, then turned to me. "I almost had the key, but I lost it." Her fist slammed against her hip. "Damn! Stupid . . ."

She sat on the hassock again, the coffee cup held in front of her, her head down. After a moment, she looked up.

"Jack Sweeney was a man with a guilty conscience," she said. "Something to do with his son and what ConEl was doing. I could sense it."

The cup rolled between her hands. Jo watched the liquid inside for a while before continuing.

"I decided to press him," she said. "I took him in my office and raked him over the coals—not once, but twice.

122

I tried to bluff him. I told him I knew everything that was going at ConEl, and I knew he was in it up to his teeth. I told him that unless he cooperated with me I would make his life miserable. I threatened tax audits, revocation of his security status—anything I could think of to put misery in his life. I said if he didn't help me convict the others, he'd go to prison with them. Finally he broke."

She put the cup on the floor and began pacing again, her hands wiping at the seams of her sweats. "The day he died, he came up to me in the employee cafeteria and told me he was ready to talk," she said. "He said he wasn't doing it to save himself, but for his son. He asked me to meet up on the roof. He used to go up there every day to think."

Jo stopped pacing and looked at me. Even in the dim light of the living room, I could see tears welling up in her eyes.

"Before I could get up there, though, he jumped," she continued. "Do you understand what that means? I pressed the man and he killed himself, *and it's my fault.*"

She covered her eyes with her hand. Her shoulders shook.

"I'm not proud of myself for that, Peter," she said.

I went to her and put my hand on her shoulder. She slipped in close to me and buried her face against my neck. My arms went around her. I couldn't help myself.

We stayed like that for a short eternity. Her tears dampened my collar. I stroked her hair. She smelled sweetly of fresh shampoo and musk perfume. I didn't know what to say, so I showed her my ace card.

"Stanning was working on some kind of black project," I told her. "Something code-named Quarry."

Jo slowly pulled away from me. Mascara streaked her face. Her eyes, reddened from crying, searched my face.

"Quarry?" she said. "I'm not familiar with any government project called Quarry, black or not."

"A source told me that," I said. "The same guy who told me about Stanning's office at ConEl."

Jo limped into the bathroom, cursed when she saw her face, and came out wiping her ruined makeup off with a tissue. She looked me, her eyes sending an icy chill though me.

"I thought you said you told me everything you knew."

I shrugged. "Now I have."

"I hope so." Limping toward the small desk, she said, "I can access ConEl's computer network from here. If there is a Project Quarry, there should be some record of it."

The tiny screen on her laptop came to life. I sat on the edge of the couch while the luminescence of the monochrome screen bathed her face. The light softened her features, made her look less tough than I knew she was. Or maybe it was just the smell of her hair and her perfume. Or maybe the memory of her crying in my arms.

"Thank you," she said stiffly.

"For what?"

"For—" She drew a breath. "For what you did for me a few minutes ago. It was very . . .kind of you."

Neither of us said anything more for several minutes as Jo accessed the ConEl computer system and searched for some clue to Project Quarry. After a while, she began shaking her head.

"There's nothing here on a project called Quarry, Peter."

"You know," I said, "the first time I heard your name, I figured you were a man. Joe with an 'e'."

"So? A lot of people do that," Jo said. "Mostly men."

"What I'm saying is this: There may be another spelling for quarry."

"How many ways can you spell quarry?"

"This is the defense industry, captain," I said. "Maybe we're dealing with an acronym. Like CCOMS."

Taking a pad and pen from the desk, I settled back into the sofa and began writing down as many phonetic spellings of quarry as I could imagine.

"Try this," I said. "Q-O-R-R-Y."

"That's pronounced 'quarry'?"

"Try it."

She tried it.

"Negative."

"Try Q-O-R-R-I."

"Nothing."

"Q-W-A-R-Y."

"Same."

"Q-W-A-R-I"

"No." Jo turned from the computer shaking her head. "Peter, I just don't think there's any Project Quarry," she said. "I think your source sold you a bill of goods."

It was my turn to shake my head.

"This is it," I said. "This has to be it."

I handed the pad to Jo. She looked at it and shrugged.

"Q-A-R-I," she read. "Why should this be it?"

"It's not an acronym," I told her. "It's an anagram."

Jo studied the pad again, then her eyes grew large with excitement.

"My God, you're right." She swung back to the computer and began typing. "It's Iraq spelled backwards."

I leaped from the couch and moved close to Jo to watch the screen. I could smell her hair, her perfume, and feel the warmth of her body. She glanced sideways at me and smiled.

"That's it," she said. "It's found something and it's accessing the files now—what?"

The words scrolling across the screen were like a door slamming shut: SECURITY PRIORITY . . . ACCESS DENIED.

Jo typed new commands into the computer and came up with the same result. She tried again, then again, each time with the same outcome. Finally, she gave up and shut down the computer.

"I don't understand this, Peter," she said, leaning back in the chair. "I'm the Pentagon security liaison. I have the highest security clearance. They can't deny me access to any government project they're working on."

"Maybe it's not a government project?" I said.

Jo marched around the living room, her fist pounding her hip. "Well, I'm going to find the hell out first thing in the morning," she said.

I watched her limp back and forth, cursing, and pounding her flesh until she had worn out her anger. Then she sat back at the computer, stretched out her bad leg, and leaned back, her head shaking.

"I'm sorry, Peter," she said. "I'm not much of a hostess."

"It's been a tough day," I said, reaching for my jacket. "We're both stressed to the max."

"You're leaving?"

I thought I heard a touch of disappointment in her voice but I disregarded it as simply my imagination.

"It's getting late," I said. "We both need to get some rest."

Jo nodded slowly, then stood clumsily. She went to the door, opened it, and leaned against its edge.

"Well, all in all," she said, "it's been a mostly pleasant evening. I mean, with the exception of finding out about being denied access. And a few other things."

I started to say good night, then I looked into her eyes and caught my breath. The ice was gone. She looked almost frightened. Her lips drew mine like a magnet to metal. I kissed her once, softly. Her mouth parted and she didn't pull rank, so I kissed her again, a little harder. Her arms went around my neck and mine around her waist. The door seemed to shut by itself, and the next thing I knew we were like teenagers in heat.

By the time we reached the bedroom, we had left a trail clothes. But it stopped right there. Suddenly, with only her sweat pants left to remove, Jo froze. Her hands grabbed mine as they played with the elastic waistband and pulled them away. I looked at her.

"I'm sorry," she said. "You're the first since..." Her head dipped in embarrassment. "My wound. I'm afraid you won't like me."

I kissed her forehead, then her eyes, her nose and finally her mouth. I went to her neck and worked my lips across her shoulder and down. She had an athlete's body, strong and supple. Her skin was tight yet soft, and sweetly scented. Her breasts were small but full. Their dark nipples stiffened as I kissed them. I kneeled before her and worked my mouth across the plain of her belly. This time she didn't stop me as I slipped the sweats and panties down her legs. She stepped out of them and turned her bad leg away from me.

The curve of her buttocks and the slender length of her left leg were as perfect as the rest of her body. But in the dressing mirror, I glimpsed what she was hiding. A jagged scar marred her leg from hip to mid-thigh, surrounded by smaller pockmarks I recognized as shrapnel wounds. The scars were still pink, still healing. A patch of darker skin revealed a burn covered by a skin graft.

I turned her around and caressed her wound. She tried to stop me, but I forced her hand away and gently kissed the scarring. Then I stood, took her hand, and ran her fingers across the scar above my eye. She smiled and relaxed.

"Damaged goods," she said. "Both of us."

I nodded and she led me to the bed.

We made love as if we hadn't had the chance to do so in a lifetime. We exhausted ourselves late into the night, then closed our eyes still wrapped in each other's arms. As tired as I was, I slept only in fits. When my mind did succumb to exhaustion, it treated me to violent replays of the day before, the gory stage, its flag weeping blood and body parts, the cries and whimpers of the hurt and wounded.

I woke in a cold sweat and could still hear whimpering. Jo was gone from my side, but not far away. She sat on the edge of the bed, her faced buried in her hands, sobbing. I touched her shoulder and she turned and threw herself into my arms, still crying.

"I'm sorry," she sobbed. "I had a nightmare."

"About yesterday?"

Her head shook against my shoulder.

"About over there," she said. "What happened . . . to us."

"The war? How you got wounded?"

"It was so horrible," she said. "I can't seem to forget it at all. It just keeps coming back. I can never sleep anymore."

"I know," I said, stroking her hair. "I know."

She pulled back and looked at me. Tears streaked her face. The wet trails shimmered in the moon light filtering through the window.

"Does it ever go away?" she asked.

"I've been told it does."

"You believe it?"

I pulled her close to me again and stroked her hair. I stared into a dark corner of the room and saw my own ghosts shimmering like the moonlight on her face. I decided to be honest.

"No," I told her. "I don't believe I do."

CHAPTER 13

I t was cold the next morning as I jogged the beach in Oceanside. The marine layer hugged the earth, and the surf crashed in high above the mean tide level, adding its spray to the damp fog. I had driven myself home before Jo woke, changed into my running gear, and drove the 40 miles north to Oceanside before the sun was up. To keep warm I ran sprints up and down the beach and thought of Jo.

Paul Polmar wasn't hard to spot. He wore USMC sweat pants and a Desert Storm sweatshirt with a screen print of a Cobra attack helicopter flying out of a sunset. Somewhere in his late thirties, Polmar was tall and husky, and wore his hair in the traditional Marine Corps high-and-tight crew cut. He wasn't at all surprised when I called out his name and identified myself with a business card. He studied the card while I explained the story I was doing on the Stanning suit.

"I know about the phone call you got," he said. His voice was deep and resonant. Even though he spoke low as his eyes scanned the beach for possible intruders, the captain's voice seemed to boom over the thunder of the surf.

"The man you spoke with is one of the bravest men I know," Polmar continued. "I'd fly into combat with him any day 'cause I know he'd be covering my six. His trouble is he doesn't know when to cover his own."

"Your friend said you'd talk to me about what happened that night of the friendly fire accident," I said.

Polmar smirked and looked around.

"Accident, huh?" he said. "That what they call it now?"

"It wasn't an accident?"

"Depends on who you ask and what they've got at stake," he said.

Polmar stared out to sea as if his vision could cut through the fog. His thoughts had flown miles away probably somewhere in the Iraqi desert on a night as blinding as the fog was then. In a moment, they flew back and landed where he stood.

"Look," he said. "I'll tell you what I can, but you can't quote me directly. Okay?"

I nodded and pulled a notebook and pen from the waistband of my jogging shorts. Polmar looked at the pad suspiciously, then shrugged.

"It was a two-helo mission, me and—" Polmar stopped and thought better. "The guy who called you, he was my wingman that night. I'm not going to tell you his name. He has too much to lose if you screw us over. His call sign was Dandy Two. But don't use that, either. Okay?"

"However you want it," I said.

"I was Dandy One and he was Dandy Two," Polmar continued. He turned back to stare through the fog, and fly back to that night in the desert. "It was our third mission of the day, scouting Iraqi armor. We were exhausted. We'd been through that corridor a day or so before and had a turkey shoot with their armor. I mean we just blasted them to hell. So that night we were just picking off stragglers.

"It was dark that night. Darker than I've ever seen it before. There was no moon and the smoke from the oil well fires the Eye-racks started blocked the stars out. It was so dark Starlight scopes wouldn't work. We flew by radar and searched by infrared.

"We got a call from our controllers vectoring us to an area where they had some reported Iraqi armor. We went in low with our motors muffled so we could sneak up on them. We found them. A couple of small personnel vehicles from the image on our scopes." Polmar looked at me. "And that's what you've got to understand. We never really saw them. All we could see was an image on our infrared sights."

Polmar wiped a hand across his face, then blew into his clenched fist before continuing.

"Anyway, we were told they were Eye-racks but I wasn't sure. We hadn't seen any in that area for some time, and I knew we had land units operating in there. I wanted some kind of verification. I didn't see any reason to go off half-cocked since they weren't in any position to hurt anyone and hell, a couple American A-10s had already blown up some Brit armor by mistake. I didn't want to see that happen again. I figured we could wait them out 'til morning. Our controllers didn't see it that way, though. They ordered us to take them out."

Polmar's voice grew tight. He swallowed hard a couple of times and went on.

"I could have countermanded the controller's order and I should have. I was on-scene commander. Instead, I just gave my weapons officer the okay. He locked on the lead vehicle and fired the first missile. Dandy Two fired the next. Afterward, we flew over the burning wrecks. That's when we knew. In the light from the flames we could see the inverted Vs."

The Marine officer closed his eyes and bit his lower lip. He took several deep breaths before continuing.

"I haven't had a full night's sleep since," he said. "Each night I go over it again and again in my dreams and I still can't stop the attack. I wake up in a cold sweat with that fire burning in my eyes."

"Tell me about the radio show, captain," I said.

Polmar looked at me with narrowed eyes. "How'd you know about that?"

"There was a small piece in the San Diego paper at the time," I said. "It said a Marine Corps pilot named Paul called the show and talked about a friendly fire incident no one could confirm ever happened."

Polmar nodded. His face relaxed. His cheeks puffed up and he exhaled slowly.

"I really caught hell for that. I was drunk. I'd been drinking myself to sleep for some time by then. I started listening to this radio call-in show. They were talking about friendly fire during The Storm." Polmar shook his head, his lips turned down in disgust. "A bunch of self-righteous rear echelon assholes were calling in. They didn't know what it was like out there. Next thing I realized, I was on the phone talking to this radio guy."

Polmar drew a deep breath, and let it out slowly.

"I wanted to make them understand what happened, how it could happen. What it was like operating under those conditions. All I did was shoot myself in the foot."

"Why won't the Marines confirm what happened out there that night?" I asked. "It almost sounds like a cover up."

I said it as gently as I could, but words like 'cover up' tend to raise the hackles on most interview subjects. Polmar's face hardened. His mouth twitched.

"You're going to have to get that from someone else," he said.

"What about the investigation report?"

Polmar's face didn't budge. "What investigation report?"

"There had to be an investigation into the incident," I said. "What were the conclusions?"

Polmar shook his head. "You're wrong," he said. "There is no report."

"Dandy 2 said to make you tell me about the investigation report."

Polmar's face reddened and twisted with anger.

"No fucking way, amigo," he said.

"Why not? You're the one who said you wanted to make people understand what happened out there."

"No!" It was like an explosive blast hurling all the pent up anger and invective the Marine officer stored inside himself. His voice thundered above the crash of the surf and the cries of the sea birds.

"You have to understand something," he continued. "And this you better not quote me on. I'm being drummed out of the Corps. I'm an albatross to the Pentagon or maybe someone higher. They're kicking me out as mentally unfit. They're saying I came unglued out there. They're calling it combat stress. I don't like it, but at least I'm getting my pension. I'm not going to fuck that up. I've got a wife and kids. We're going to need that money."

It was time to play hardball. Polmar was tied up tighter inside than a Tijuana Rolex, and it was time to pop the spring.

"What about the families of the men who died in those vehicles, captain?" I asked. "Don't they have the right to know what happen? What about Mrs. Stanning? At least your wife still has her husband."

I felt like a creep. I always did at this point. But the look Polmar gave me made me feel small enough to hide behind the grains of sand we stood on.

"Listen here, Brandt," he said. "What happened out there wasn't right. As far as I'm concerned, it was fucking murder. Pure and simple. But I can't afford to worry about anyone else's family. Not in this economy. I got to worry about my own."

"What'd you mean by that, captain?" I asked. "What'd you mean it was murder, pure and simple?"

"What?"

"You said it was murder."

Polmar shook his head and started to jog back the way he had come. "Get away from me, Brandt," he said over his shoulder.

I followed him up the beach a few yards, shouting against the sound of the surf and our own hard breathing.

"Is that how it goes now, captain?" I said. "Watch out for your six?" He didn't answer. He simply sped up his pace. "I don't know what happened out there that night, captain, but I've seen enough of war to know if fuck-ups aren't stopped right away, they just keep on happening. People keep on dying. But you're right, captain. You don't have to worry about it now because it won't be your ass on the line next time. But it might be your buddy's six, the guy who called me. Remember him? Dandy Two?

Your wingman who's been looking out after your six all this time?"

Polmar stopped and turned around. His face was red and I wasn't sure his heavy breathing was from running or anger.

"Just drop it, Brandt," he said. "It's not worth it."

"Whatever happened to Semper Fidelis, captain?" I asked. "Always faithful? Whatever happened to Semper Fi?"

"It died out there in the desert, Brandt," Polmar said. "That's what happened."

Then he turned and continued his run.

I walked back to the Mustang and dried myself off with a towel I'd brought along with me. I was tired physically and emotionally. As I climbed into the bucket seat, I spotted a man reading a newspaper in his car. The car was a white compact, unfamiliar. But the blue cap showing above the paper was. The driver lowered the paper and looked quizzically in my direction. He had sandy hair, light eyes, and sharp features. He watched me a moment, then went back to reading his paper.

I fired up the Mustang and pulled out. When I glanced in the rearview mirror a few minutes later, the white compact was behind me

CHAPTER 14

The message on my machine was from a man selling subscriptions to the Los Angeles Times. "For a limited time only," he said the paper was available for a reduced price and promised that I would find it "full of useful information." The man hung up without leaving a call back number or even his name. It wasn't necessary, anyway. I already subscribed to the Times, as the caller well knew. Second, I'd recognize Fred Danbury's Texas drawl anywhere.

I didn't bother changing out of my jogging clothes. I grabbed a handful of change and, as Fred and I had arranged, walked down to the beach and called him on a pay phone.

"The first thing, Pete," Fred said, "is Project Quarry ain't spelled the way you told me. Not that I'd expect any idiot reporter to get anything accurate."

I could imagine Fred Danbury's rock-hard face twisted in a sardonic grin, the sharply angled salt-and-pepper moustache pointing even steeper toward the ground, and just a hint of a glint in the normally dark and cold eyes. I had met Fred when I was working down South covering the fighting in Nicaragua. He had been with General Singlaub's group of anti-communists doing the work they thought the U.S. government should have been doing. An ex-CIA pilot, Fred was training Contra pilots how to fly heavily loaded cargo planes dangerously low to the ground so their kickers could drop parachuted supplies with pinpoint accuracy to Contra fighters, just as Fred had done to CIA mercenaries in Vietnam, Cambodia and Laos. He was big man, well over six-foot, with a taste for Jack Daniels and a distaste for journalists unless a journalist was willing to listen to his war stories and his rhetoric without judgment and pay for the privilege of doing so by keeping the Jack Daniels flowing.

"Oh, didn't I tell you that, Fred?" I lied. "Q-A-R-I. Like Iraq, but spelled backwards. Sorry."

I heard a growl from the other end of the line, then the flick of a cigarette lighter probably lighting one of the small, tightly rolled cigars Fred loved.

"Yeah? Well, anyway," he said, "I know this guy with the Company. Knew him in Saigon when I was flying for Air America and he was just a young pup fresh from Arlington. Now he's head of ops for the Middle East. This guy says he knows all about this Qari thing, but he couldn't talk to me about it 'cept to tell me two things."

Fred paused to take a long puff on his cigar. I could hear him breathe in then exhale luxuriously. Fred always had talent for dramatic timing.

"All right, Fred," I said. "What were they?"

Fred chuckled before continuing. "One," he said, "the Company wasn't involved. Fact is, he says they were dead set against it whatever it was. The other thing he said was there are two players down on your turf who could tell you about Qari if they were willing to talk about it. One's a Customs agent who was involved in busting some Iraqis trying to smuggle nuclear bomb parts to Baghdad a couple years ago."

I had my pad out and scribbled notes.

"Name?"

"He didn't give it," Fred said. "Christ, Pete, I can't do all your work for you."

"Thanks, Fred. The second guy?"

"That one my friend was more than willing to name. Roger Sherman. United States Air Force retired."

"Sherman?"

"You know him?"

"I've met him," I said. "He works for ConEl now."

Fred grunted. "I've met him, too," he said. "He was working with Ollie North down South on the Contra screw up. He was Air Force special operations, like Dick Secord. I heard he got passed over for promotion to general for that and got banished to procurement until he could retire."

"He told me he just started working at ConEl a few months ago."

"Way I hear it, Sherman would've been processed out a lot sooner 'cept Desert Storm came along. But as soon as the fighting stopped, he was shown the door. My friend says Sherman had some baggage on him the Air Force wanted to distance itself from."

"Project Qari?"

"Could be," Fred said. I could almost see his sardonic smile again. "That's what you're supposed to find out, Mr. Reporter." Fred was still chuckling as the line when dead.

§

Michael Larrs had what the TV news business calls good timing. Not only did he deliver the news in an authoritative voice with good measure and a flair for the dramatic, he knew when to grab hold of a news event and ride it for what it was worth. He was as much a celebrity for his nightly commentaries—three spite-filled minutes he called his perspectives—and the legend he had built around his career as he was for his news reporting. But I knew his legend was all myth, that he claimed as his own the hard work of other reporters who didn't have the bully pulpit that enabled Larrs to focus attention on himself. Besides, I thought his timing stunk, just as it did that day.

Larrs rapped at my door just as I was getting out of the shower. I'd been back from my phone call with Fred Danbury for less than thirty minutes, just time enough to call Jo, pass along what Fred had passed on to me, and to shave and shower. I quickly rubbed the towel over myself, pulled on a pair of jeans and padded to the door in my bare feet. My stomach growled for breakfast and I needed another cup of coffee.

"What are you doing here?" I asked, glaring at Larrs through the screen door.

He looked like a mannequin in a tailored gray pinstripe suit, a red Yves St. Laurent tie flawlessly knotted and snugged up against his Adam's apple, and with hair combed as perfectly straight as the pinstripes on his suit. He smiled, rubbed his ear, and looked around the neighborhood. His finely manicured nails glistened with varnish. A gold Rolex glittered on his wrist.

"You know, Brandt," he said. "They'd probably let you into a better neighborhood if you'd learn some social graces."

"Funny, I was wondering who let *you* into this neighborhood."

"Witty as ever," Larrs said. "Are you going to invite me in or are we going to talk through this screen door? I didn't even know they made screen doors anymore."

The screen door creaked as I pushed it open. I made certain to bump it into Larrs and leave a trace of dust on his tailored suit. Larrs brushed it off as he glanced around the front room, his mouth puckered in distaste.

"So what'd you do, Larrs?" I asked. "Make a wrong turn on the way to La Jolla and end up in Ocean Beach?"

Larrs walked casually past my desk, not so casually examining the papers there.

"I came to offer you a business deal," he said. "I found your address in the press club directory."

"I knew I should have listed my P.O. box."

"Is that coffee I smell?"

"Yes."

He stood looking at me in silence, just smiling with his capped teeth.

"Oh, all right," I finally said. "Milk or sugar?"

"Black with sweetener, if you've got it," he said. "Got to watch my figure, you know."

I detoured to the bedroom and pulled on shoes and a shirt. I poured the coffee, sweetened Larrs', and walked out of the kitchen to find the son of a bitch going through my desk.

"What the hell are you doing?"

Larrs jumped like a boy found rummaging through his father's drawer of *Playboy*s. His mouth open and shut fishlike. Then his composure returned and he slipped one hand into his pocket and reached out with the other.

"Oh, coffee's ready so soon?"

He grabbed the cup before I could submit to the urge to throw it in his face.

"Again," I said. "What the hell were you doing going through my desk?"

Larrs sipped the coffee, made a face, then paced the floor.

"Okay," he said. "This is why I'm really here "

"I thought you said you were going to offer me a business deal."

"Oh, yeah, right," he stammered. "I am. I am." Larrs paced the floor some more, then stopped at the desk and eyed the papers there some more. "I've been curious about why Peter Brandt has been at ConEl both times someone's died there in the last few days."

"I guess I'm just bad luck," I said. "Must be some kind of Jonah."

"No." Larrs let the word roll slowly off his tongue, smiling with his nice white caps. He shook his head slowly. "I don't think so. See, I've got a source at ConEl and he tells me a reporter has been asking around about some lawsuit supposedly filed against the company by the widow of a guy named Stanning. Funny thing, though, nobody knows anything about the suit. I went downtown and checked both the federal court and the county court there's no such suit in the indexes. So I'm thinking: What's Brandt up to? It's got to be something good."

Larrs looked at me, waiting for me to respond. I stared back over the rim of my coffee cup.

"Come on, Brandt, at least tell me who you're working for." Larrs waited in vain again. "I know you've been doing some writing for *San Diego Life*. Are you on assignment for them?"

Larrs answered the question himself. "That's it, isn't it?" He raised his eyes to the ceiling and shook his head. "Christ, Brandt, they can't pay you shit. I'll more than match it, whatever it is."

"You don't even know what it is," I said.

"Hey, I know your work," Larrs said. "You don't dabble in the small stuff. There's something going on at ConEl. My own source tells me that, but he doesn't know what it is. I'm betting you do. Come on, we'll share the credit, you and I."

I nearly snorted the hot coffee through my nose. "Sure, Larrs," I said. "You don't share the credit with anyone. I'd think that little incident with the mayor would have stopped you from filching other reporter's stories."

"You owe me for that, Brandt."

"I told you before," I said. "I don't owe you shit."

Larrs placed his cup on the desk and straightened his coat.

"Fine," he said. "Have it your way. But I'm going to find out what it is, Brandt. You can make a hell of a lot more money working with me than you can writing for that rag. Think about it."

I opened the screen door for Larrs, and made sure to bump him with it again. The dust it left nicely matched his pinstripes.

CHAPTER 15

Larrs' visit left an ugly taste in my mouth which I
desperately wanted to burn away with a cigarette.
Instead, I drank more coffee, ate some cereal, got
into the Mustang, and burned rubber as I tore out of my
driveway and headed toward La Jolla and the university.

The morning overcast brought with it a chill, and the
coeds were disappointingly dressed for warmth. As I
walked across campus, I entertained myself instead with
memories of Jo and the love we had made the night
before. But there was something scratching at the back of
my mind, and it kept distracting me from my indulgence.
Instead of visions of Jo's naked form lying in bed, I kept
seeing Jack Sweeney's crushed body bleeding on the
sidewalk. I began to wonder about myself.

It was too early for most college kids to study. The
library was empty except for the librarians and a handful
of nerdy students who probably had never stayed up late
for a beer bust in their lives. I quickly found a computer
station, laid out my notepad, and logged on to the
newspaper database.

I knew the Customs case Fred Danbury had
mentioned. It would have been difficult to ignore it. Just

months before Saddam marched his troops into Kuwait, several of his agents were arrested in London after picking up a shipping crate full of American-made nuclear bomb detonators. The detonators were dummies, sent to them by an U.S. Customs agent who had duped them into believing he was a dishonest businessman. The arrests made headlines the world over.

But that was all I remembered about the story. It took me thirty minutes scanning the electronic newspaper morgue to refresh my memory of case details. It took another half hour of searching to find a story that listed the undercover agent's name.

Back at my apartment, I called the U.S. Customs office downtown and asked for Special Agent Dick Sanders. The operator put me right through. By the sound of Sanders' voice, I'd say he wasn't happy about that.

"Sorry, I don't talk to reporters, Mr.—" Sanders was talking on a speakerphone. His words echoed through the line. He paused and I could hear a desk drawer open and close. "What's your name again?" I told him again and could hear a pen scratching on paper.

"Phil Kolby knows me," I said. "He can vouch for me."

"Phil Kolby's no longer SIC," Sanders said. I detected the trace of a New York accent. "He retired two years ago."

"Good for him," I said. "But bad for me. He could have vouched for me. He helped me on some stories years ago."

"Yeah, too freaking bad," Sanders said. "Just why do you want to talk to me?"

I told him the truth. Or most of it. I told him about the magazine assignment, the death of Robert Stanning and his widow's lawsuit. I didn't tell him about the lawsuit disappearing from the court records office, or about Jo's belief that Stanning was selling arms to the Iraqis. We all have to keep our little secrets.

"What's that got to do with me?"

"I understand Stanning was working on something called Project Qari when he was killed," I said. "That mean anything to you?"

"Not a fucking thing. How's that spelled?"

"Q-A-R-I," I said. "Like Iraq backwards. I was told by a source you'd know about Project Qari."

"What kind of source?"

I stretched the truth a bit. "CIA."

Sanders let go a loud laugh. "Sure it wasn't James fucking Bond?" He laughed some more then said: "Look, Brandt. I don't know anything about this Project Qari of yours, and if I did I probably couldn't tell you about it anyway. Sorry."

By speaking very fast, I managed to leave my phone number before he hung up.

§

My hand wasn't even off the receiver when the phone rang. I snatched it up, expecting to hear Sanders' New York accent. It was Jo Rice, instead. I didn't feel too disappointed about that.

"I think I know a good place to talk to Sherman," she said. "He takes a late lunch each day so he can work out in the gym alone. I think we should be able to talk to him in private there."

"We?"

"I'd like to talk to him, too," she said. "I thought we were going to work at this as a team. Or were all those sweet things you told me last night just lies to get me in bed?"

Her voice was teasing, pleasing.

"You misunderstood," I teased back. "I was talking about another kind of team work."

"He works out at three," Jo said. "I'll leave a pass for you at the gate and meet you outside the gym. Maybe we can discuss your ideas about team work after we talk to Sherman."

I hadn't heard that kind of sultriness in Jo's voice before. It echoed in my ears long after she hung up.

§

For several minutes, I stared out the window at the sunlit trees beyond, admiring the colors of the leaves and enjoying the flitting of the finches in the limbs. I wondered at how things could look so different the morning after. Hormones, I guessed. Then I started thinking about Jack Sweeney again, and really began worrying about myself. Finally, I picked up the phone and dialed police headquarters downtown. It took a few minutes to get patched through to the right desk in homicide.

"McCarty."

The voice at the other end had the distinct ability to make you think it had just said, "Hey, dude," without actually saying it. At forty-five, Mike McCarty still looked like the surfer he had been in high school and college. His hair was shaggy and sun-bleached. So was his moustache. Each morning, Mike shot the curls off La

Jolla for an hour before going to work. During the summers, he moonlighted part-time as a city lifeguard. When he wasn't curling his toes in beach sand, he was a lieutenant of homicide.

"Hey, Mike," I said. "Peter Brandt."

"Hey, dude. What's up?"

"Looked like the surf was up this morning when I jogged."

"Maybe where you were, man," Mike said. "Where I was it was anything but tubular."

"Groddy, man," I said.

"Learn the lingo if you're going to use it, Pete."

"Far out? Way in? Frankie and Annette?"

"Forget it," Mike said. "Is this a pleasure call or business?"

"Business. *I think.*"

"You think?"

I took a deep breath and organized my lies before telling them. I watched a mommy finch stuff her over-fluffed baby with food on one of the tree limbs. The baby's wings fluttered with each tasty morsel.

"Well, one part's business, the other's curiosity."

"Better start with the business part, then."

"I think I'm being followed."

"Go on."

"A couple cars seem to be tailing me everywhere I've gone for the past week."

"Not familiar? Not someone you know?"

"No."

"Pissed off reader?"

"Could be. I don't know. But I got the license number of one of them. I wondered if you could check it out."

"You willing to file a complaint?"

"I don't know. Maybe."

"Can't run a plate if you don't file a complaint," Mike said. "I'd get my balls tied in a knot."

The mother bird and her baby flew off as a jetliner roared over on its way out to sea. I let the windows stop shaking before answering.

"Okay," I said. "If it turns up anything, I'll file a complaint."

"Okay," Mike said. "What's the number?"

I gave it to him and I heard the clacking of computer keys.

"This'll take a little while," Mike said. "System's busy."

"That's okay," I said.

"So what's the curiosity part?"

"I was wondering what you make of the jumper at ConEl the other day," I told him. "Jack Sweeney."

"Is this for a story?"

"Not really," I said, hedging. "I was there working on a story when he jumped. I was just curious."

"Not a happy place, ConEl," Mike said. "First the layoffs, then Sweeney nose dives, then the sniper thing. Not a happy place."

"I was there when that happened, too," I said.

"The shooting?" I grunted in the affirmative. "They must like you there a lot."

"I'm beginning to feel like Jonah," I said. "Guess I need to buy a new rabbit's foot. Tell me about Sweeney's leap."

"Maybe you should ask me if he did leap."

"Like maybe he didn't?"

"Well, maybe, maybe not," Mike said. "Normally when someone jumps, they just sort of step off and fall real close to the foot of the building or the bridge or whatever. Sweeney's body fell so far from the foot of the building, it looked like he took a running start. Bogus, man."

"And that means?" Alarm bells were going off in my head. I now knew why the memory of Sweeney's nosedive kept knocking at the back of my mind.

"Well, normally that means he may have been pushed or thrown. But not always."

"Okay," I said. "Cut to the chase, Mike. What's your guess on this?"

"Well, we understand Sweeney had been pretty badly depressed recently. Seems his son was a fighter jock and got dusted over Baghdad. Sweeney took it hard. My guess is he probably jumped."

"Probably?"

"Probably," Mike said. "But it's not the kind of guess I'd be willing to bet money on. *Jesus Christ—*"

"What?"

"What kind of shit are you into, Pete?"

"What is it?"

"This plate comes back as unregistered," Mike said. "I don't like this."

"Mike, how about letting me in on it?"

"If those plates were real, they'd be in the database," the detective said.

"What do you mean, if they were real?" I asked.

"I'm not sure," Mike said, now whispering into the phone. "But I heard about something like this a few years ago. Some guys down in narcotics had an East County rural airfield under surveillance. Thought it was being used to fly in drugs. A couple of the vehicles videotaped had plates that didn't exist. They turned out to be feds."

"FBI? DEA?"

"Spooks, Pete," Mike said. "Some kind of ultra-secret spooks. We never really learned who. But right after we ran the plates, they shut down our investigation real fast. I mean real fast."

"Who was working that case, Mike?"

"Who?"

"Yeah. Was it Lt. Holden in the street team?"

"Yeah, that's right," he said. "But he wasn't with the street team then. He was doing major cases. Why?"

"Just a guess."

I sighed heavily. The detective echoed my sigh.

"Well, listen. I gotta go, dude," he finally said. "If I'm right, these creeps are maxing their RPMs right now getting here to do me over. Later, dude."

The line clicked dead. The colors outside the window seemed to dim. I stared instead at the blank computer screen on my desk. It began to make sense and yet make no sense at all. Whoever was following me had planted that brick of grass in my toilet and snitched to Holden. I could almost hear the conversation. *Remember how we screwed up that case of yours before, Holden? Well, here's some payback. You can pin this guy Brandt. He's holding big.*

I understood now how Susan Stanning's lawsuit was sealed and all traces of it removed from court records, how Stanning's existence at ConEl had been sanitized, even how Paul Polmar's deadly mistake on the battlefield had been buried. I could see the how; what I couldn't see was the why. Or the way Jack Sweeney's suicide fitted into it—if, indeed, it was suicide. The earpiece of the telephone receiver hadn't even cooled when the phone rang again. It was Dick Sanders.

"Kolby remembers you," he said. "He thinks I should talk with you. Meet me outside the deli at Horton Plaza at five."

The line went dead before I could even agree.

CHAPTER 16

The inland sun made a mockery of the coastal overcast. The ConEl parking lot shimmered with the heat. The grass of the athletic field curled and turned brown. Jo waited for me in the shade of the gymnasium, dressed sharply in her Class A's, her hair tucked up beneath the beret. She didn't seem to notice how warm it was.

"So did your meeting go okay this morning?" she asked.

I thought about kissing her and leaned toward her to do the deed, but she pulled away sharply, her eyes darting back and forth. Her hand quickly squeezed mine and she whispered, "Not here."

"Your meeting?" she asked again.

"Which meeting?"

"The one that tore you away from my bed so early this morning. There was a meeting, wasn't there?" She casually bumped my shoulder and glanced at me from the corner of her eye. "Or was that an excuse to not have to look me in the eye after the dirty deed?"

"Was it so dirty?"

"Nasty is more like it," she said, smiling slyly. "Your meeting?"

"I managed to charm another prospective source with my insolence and sly wit," I said, then told her about my meeting with Paul Polmar. She plied me with a dozen or more questions, and when I finished the smile was gone from her face and her eyes seemed just as far away.

"There was something else I found out," I said. She didn't seem to hear. I repeated it.

"What?" she said, coming back from wherever she had been. "What was that?"

"About Jack Sweeney," I said. "I talked to someone I know in homicide. He said there were some peculiarities about Sweeney's death." I turned to face her and put my hand on her shoulder. "Jo, Sweeney may not have jumped. It's possible—just possible—he may have been pushed."

Jo stared at me long and hard as I told her what Mike McCarty had said. I knew it wasn't much. It probably wasn't even true. But if it gave her the slightest doubt about her own guilt, it might give her room enough to forgive herself.

When I finished, she bit her lower lip and turned away.

"So it's just *maybe* he was pushed," she said. "Nothing definite."

"Just maybe," I said quietly.

After a while, she turned back to me and gave my hand squeeze.

"Thank you, Peter," she said. Then she fixed her face, straightened her tunic, and said, "Shall we go talk to the mysterious Colonel Sherman?"

§

The ConEl gymnasium could have passed as a commercial fitness center. There was an Olympic-size pool, two hot tubs and two saunas, a weight room with free weights and machines, racquetball courts, a place for aerobics classes, and a large open room crowded with stationary bikes, step machines and treadmills, all lined up like little soldiers. All of it was air-conditioned and all of it, no doubt, was paid for with tax dollars. But with the layoffs, there were too few employees left to make full use of the facilities. The gym was as empty as a warehouse during a Teamster strike.

We found Roger Sherman alone in the weight room, sweating through an Air Force Academy T-shirt and shorts as he cranked out reps on the bench press. The barbell was loaded with more weight than I could count quickly, and the muscles in his arms bulged as he strained through the last of the presses. When he finished, he sat up and wiped the sweat from his face with a small towel. His eyes were as black as coal as he watched us approach.

"Well, Captain Rice, the Pentagon watchdog," Sherman said. A smile creased his face and bared his teeth. He reminded me of a wolf. "Working out today or making sure no one has stolen the free weights?"

"Colonel Sherman," Jo said coolly. She nodded in my direction. "You've met Peter Brandt."

Sherman wiped his right hand and held it out. "I have?"

"A few days ago in the conference room with David Brooks," I said, shaking his hand.

Sherman's eyes showed no recognition, but he conceded the fact.

"Yes, of course," he said. "You're a reporter, doing a story on . . . CCOMS, right?"

"Actually, on the defense cuts and ConEl's layoffs," I said, slipping back into my pretext.

"Well, now you can see the impact," Sherman said, waving about the room. He picked up a curl bar and added weights to it. "Used to be you had to stand in line to use the weights or a machine. Now look. I have it practically to myself. Terrible."

"You don't agree with the military downsizing?" I asked.

Sherman eyed me suspiciously. "This for your story?" He started doing arm curls.

"Maybe," I said. "It's impacted you, hasn't it?"

Sherman finished ten curls and set the bar down. "It's impacted a lot of people . . . Peter, isn't it?"

I nodded and waited for him to finish another ten curls.

"Far too many people," he continued. "It's a tragedy, really."

"The layoffs, you mean?"

Sherman completed another set of ten curls, then wiped his face again. He moved on to the squat stand, added weights and positioned himself on the platform.

"Certainly the layoffs," he said before dipping for the first of a set of twenty squats. The muscles in his thighs strained beneath his shorts and his cheeks puffed with air. His eyes remained steady, black pits.

"You think the downsizing was a mistake?"

Sherman stepped away from the squat station, wiping his face and bald head, his eyes studying me. They reminded me of the working end of a double-barreled shotgun. He finally turned away to study the dumbbell racks.

"Off the record, Pete." He picked out a set of fifty pounders and settled down on an inclined bench. "Sure it's mistake. It's still a dangerous world, Soviet Union or no Soviet Union. Saddam Hussein showed us that."

Jo looked at me curiously while Sherman completed a set of flies. I just smiled at her and nodded.

"Still a dangerous world," Sherman repeated as he set the weights down.

"I'll tell you, Colonel Sherman," I said. "I'm more interested in the personal impact than the international perspective. Yourself, for instance. I understand you were a victim of the Pentagon downsizing."

Sherman shot a glance at me. The crevices around his mouth deepened.

"I'm retired, Pete," he said. He seated himself at the lat pull-down. "I did my time and got out with my pension. Actually, I would've retired sooner, but Desert Storm got in the away."

Sherman began his set of pull-downs, his face and muscles straining with each repetition. I waited for him to finish a set of twenty before continuing.

"But you were on a fast track to general, weren't you?" I asked. Sherman's black pits bored through me. He didn't answer. "At least until the cutbacks, right?" Still nothing. "Or did your involvement with Iran-Contra put the brakes on your career? Or maybe Project Qari?"

Sherman kept his eyes on me as he did twenty more lats. Jo's eyes flitted between the colonel and me. When he finished, Sherman wiped off again before speaking.

"Iran-Contra?"

"I mean, I know you were involved with North and Secord in the delivery of missiles to Iran to free the hostages? Right? I remember that from the hearings. That must've put a black mark on your record. You didn't make general after that, am I right?'

"I was simply part of an operation I was ordered to take part in." Sherman rose from the lat station, never taking his eyes from mine. "There were no repercussions from what I did. It may have been a screwup, but that happens in the fog of war. And I was under orders."

"I didn't know we were at war with Iran," I said. "Or was it Nicaragua? I always get confused."

"We're always at war, Mr. Brandt," Sherman said, wrapping the towel around his neck. "There may not be gunfire or battlefields, but there are national interests at stake that must be protected. Like I said, it's still a dangerous world."

Sherman and I were thrusting and parrying, and getting absolutely nowhere. He took my bluff and threw it back in my face. If Project Qari meant anything to Sherman, he was doing a damn good job of hiding it. I looked at Jo. She raised her eyebrows. I decided on a more straightforward tact.

"You're absolutely right, colonel," I said. "I seem to have gotten off track. I'll be honest with you now, sir. I actually came to ask you about the late Robert Stanning. But since everyone seems so sensitive about discussing him, I thought I'd just sort of guide the conversation in that direc—"

"I told you, Mr. Brandt. I never knew Stanning."

"Yes, you said that, colonel. But I've since found out that you and Stanning both worked on Project Qari, so you must have known him."

The muscles in Sherman's face formed tight little knots. The veins in his neck ballooned out. The coal in his eyes turned to fiery embers.

"Don't tell me what I must have known, Brandt," Sherman said. He adjusted the towel around his neck and stepped into my face, his feet apart, one hand planted firmly on his waist, the other poking an index finger in my chest. "I don't have to take this shit from you. I don't have to talk to you, period. The last time I checked, this was still a free country."

"You don't have to talk to Peter, colonel, but you do have to talk to me."

Sherman and I both turned toward Jo. She stood ramrod straight and there was enough frost in her blue eyes to put out the embers in Sherman's coal-fire eyes.

"I don't think so," Sherman hissed.

"I'm the Pentagon security officer here, colonel," Jo said, her voice tight. "If you have information bearing on the death of Robert Stanning, I need to know it."

The embers died in Sherman's eyes. The lines around his mouth deepened and bent. He started laughing.

"I think not, sweetie," he said. "They may let you wear that uniform, but don't take it too seriously."

Sherman walked up to Jo and slipped the towel from his neck. He leaned into her and spoke in a voice that couldn't hold more contempt than it already did.

"There's more to this work than just wearing that uniform, captain," he said. He shook his head slowly. "And they don't let little girls do the real work. Just remember that."

Sherman stepped past Jo, turned, and snapped her ass with the towel. Jo would have launched into him if I hadn't grabbed her. Sherman walked away laughing loudly and disappeared into the men's locker room. We could still hear his laughter as we left the gym.

CHAPTER 17

I gunned the Mustang through Mission Valley, took the southbound exit to the I-5 and got off at the first downtown exit. The other cars on the freeways flashed past in a blur of color and glinting chrome and windows. My mind was elsewhere.

It took Jo nearly half an hour to calm down. I walked her out of the gymnasium, around the dying athletic field and, finally, out to the parking lot and my car. By the time we reached the Mustang, she had vented her rage and winded herself with an unending string of epithets hurled at the world in general and Roger Sherman in particular. As we stood at the car, we both started laughing.

"Damn, that felt good," Jo said. She leaned against the roof of the Mustang, her fingers caressing her forehead, curls of blonde hair falling from her beret. "That smug, self-righteous son-of-a-bitch."

"Don't get started again," I warned. "I don't think my ears can take much more abuse."

"I'm sorry, Peter." She looked at me and her eyes were large and warm. Not an icicle to be seen. "I don't know. It was like he was . . ."

"Your father?"

"Right."

Jo sagged against the car and shook her head.

"We didn't learn much despite all that, did we?"

"Not much," I said. "But some."

"Like what?"

She looked at me with her head tilted, her lips pursed. I wanted very much to kiss her.

"Sometimes in an interview, it's not as important what they say as it is what they don't say," I told her. That only made her furrow her brow. "He never acknowledged my asking him about Project Qari."

Jo shook her head and pursed her lips more. "I don't understand."

"If he had never heard of Project Qari, why not say so? Your normal reaction would be to ask, 'Project what?'" I shook my head and looked around. The sun was beginning to hurt my eyes and head. I took the aviators from my pocket and put them on. "I asked him twice about Qari and he wouldn't take the bait. He sidestepped it."

"But he denied knowing Stanning."

"Because he had already told that lie to me," I said. "He had to stay the course. And the stuff about Iran-Contra has been a matter of public record for years."

"So what's it mean? He does know something about Qari?"

I shrugged. "I don't know what it means," I said. "But he got upset only after I mentioned Qari. My guess is he knows more than a little about it. Just as my source told me."

"Well, that's certainly something, isn't it?"

Jo straightened and smiled. She adjusted her tunic and tucked the stray strands of hair back into the beret. Then she stood there looking at me, waiting.

"I guess I'd better get back to the office," she said finally.

I glanced at me watch. "Yeah, I've got to get going, too."

Jo looked at me some more. I looked back. She took a deep breath and let it out.

"Peter, when I said 'not here' earlier . . ."

"Yes?"

"I didn't mean *not here*."

I smiled and put my arms around her and kissed her long and hard. When I stopped, I must have looked at her strangely.

"Something wrong?" she asked.

"It just kind of feels funny kissing an army captain," I said. "It must be the uniform."

"Shut up and kiss me."

It was an order, and like a good soldier, I obeyed.

§

The recession had cleared the parking garage at Horton Plaza as it had most retail centers. I had my choice of spots in the grape, orange or banana levels. I chose the banana level. I like bananas. The sign on the wall near the elevator warned me to remember my fruit. Easy. Hey, mister, is that a banana in your parking slot or are you happy to see me?

Horton Plaza is the retail version of Disneyland, an outdoor mall surrounded by brightly colored peaked roofs and staggered levels of shops and restaurants. It took architectural daring to build the plaza in a city not used to derring-do, but before the recession, it was an astounding success. It was doing okay now, too, but, from the number of closed shops, it wasn't doing great.

The deli where Sanders wanted to meet was on the far side of the plaza on the ground level. It was also directly across the street from the office building housing Customs' Office of Investigations. I bought a cup of coffee and sat at a table outside where I could watch the foot traffic coming from that direction. Even then, I didn't realize I was looking at the undercover agent until he was standing at my table.

"You Brandt?"

It was the voice and the New York accent I recognized. Dick Sanders stood at average height with average weight and had a youthful but average face that would have fit well on a choirboy or Billy the Kid. He was in his mid or late thirties with short, dark, curly hair graying at the temples. He was dressed in conservative business attire, with a gold Rolex and a matching wrist bracelet.

"Nice watch," I said as he sat down. "We must pay you civil servants better these days."

He had a grin like a New York homeboy. "Don't you believe it," he said. "I had a meet with a suspect this morning. This stuff's all flash. It goes back into the government safe when I finish this assignment. Let me get some coffee."

He came back with a steaming Styrofoam cup and a quizzical look on his face. He sat back down and stared over my shoulder with a knitted brow.

"Sorry about meeting here instead of my office," he finally said. "They don't like me talking about the Iraqi case anymore."

"They?" I prodded.

"Everyone," he answered.

"Why's that?"

"It was . . ." Sanders smirked, "an embarrassment to certain people in our government."

"What do you mean by that?" I asked.

Sanders looked around, the Styrofoam cup twirling between the fingers of both hands. "How much do you know about the case I worked on?"

"What I read in the papers."

Again, the New York smirk. "That was nothing," he said. "That was just what they wanted people to know."

"Does this have to do with Qari?"

Sanders focused on me now, his eyes squinting. "Just how much do you know about Qari?"

"Enough."

I never thought a Styrofoam cup could be slammed down, but Sanders did a convincing imitation of just that. Coffee spilled out and beaded on the white tabletop. It shimmered in the sunlight, like black mercury.

"Let's get something fucking straight here," Sanders said. "This is a two-way street. You give a little, I give a little. But you start the giving."

So I told him what I knew about Robert Stanning's involvement in Qari, how I believed that involvement had something to do with his being in Iraq during Desert Storm, how the project had some incredibly high-level security attached to it, and how I believed Susan Stanning's lawsuit was seen as a threat to whatever Qari was. Sanders shot a couple of questions across the table, but when I finished with my tale, he seemed satisfied.

Now it was his turn to give a little, I told him.

Sanders nodded and sipped what was left of his coffee, his eyes flitting from me to something behind me. I fought the urge to turn around.

"Okay," he said. "You know the basics of the case. The Iraqis tried to get a local company to build them some detonators for nuclear bombs. Of course, they didn't tell the company what they were. They just gave them the specs and said they were for scientific research. Only one of the company execs used to work for the Energy Department—you know, the guys who build our bombs—and he recognized the specs. They were identical to a type of detonator used in one of our warheads. So this company calls Customs, I get brought in undercover as one of the company execs, and I infiltrate the Iraqis. I start dealing with them over the phone, holding meets with them here and in London. Got them to trust me, start talking about what they really wanted. Jesus, by the time I finished with them, they gave me a fucking shopping list of bomb parts and technology three fucking pages long."

Sanders rubbed his chin, smiling and shaking his head. He sipped from the foam cup again before continuing.

"Dealing with the rag-heads was easy," he said. "Dealing with our own fucking government—that's where it got dicey."

"What do you mean by dicey?"

"We couldn't get any support from Washington," he said. "It was like they simply didn't care. Then as the case progressed, it wasn't just lack of support we got, it was goddamn obstruction."

He drank a little of the coffee then flicked a finger at me.

"Let me give you an example," he said. "I'm not an engineer. I wouldn't know a detonator from a tire pump if all I have are specs for them. So I sent copies of the spec sheet the rag-heads gave this company to three national laboratories and simply asked them to tell me what they were for. I sent another copy to British Customs and another to the State Department. Within a week, all three labs and the Brits got back to me saying they were the specs for a nuclear detonator. State didn't get back to me for six fucking months, and when they did they said they didn't know what the fuck the specs were for, they weren't on the Munitions List, and there was no fucking reason to continue our investigation."

"The Munitions List," I said. "That's the list of weapons-related technology that can't be exported, right?"

"Basically." Sanders nodded, but went on without further correction. "Anyway, that was just the beginning. After a while, State started coming down hard on us, demanding we stop the investigation or at least delay it. Commerce, too. And when those two cabinet departments are involved, you know the White House is, too. But, Kolby was retiring. He said fuck this shit, and told me to go for it. And I did."

"They say why they wanted you to stop?"

"Of course not," Sanders said, shaking his head. "They never have to explain anything they do. They're too fucking important. Didn't you know that?"

Sanders smiled his tough hood smile and waited for me to grin back. Then he looked down at his cup. "I need some more java," he said. "You?"

"I'll get it." I took the cups and refilled in the deli. When I came back, Sanders was just sitting back down in his chair with a peculiar grin on his face. He took the coffee and thanked me. I thought I saw a humorous glint in his eye.

"Anyway, where was I?"

"The State and Commerce departments were blocking your investigation."

"Good, you've been listening," he said. "So this investigation went on a year and a half, you understand? We started learning it was much bigger than this one group of rag-heads in England looking for detonators. They were everywhere. All through Europe, even here in the States. And looking for anything they could get their hands on dealing with unconventional weaponry—not just nukes, but ballistic missiles, nerve gas, you name it.

"And from what we could tell, they were getting it. Everybody was selling whatever they could to Iraq. The rag-heads even bought companies here in the States to act as fronts for them. We found out about them, but we weren't allowed to take them down."

"Why's that?"

"What do I have to do, Brandt? Paint you a fucking picture?"

"I wish you would," I said. "I wish someone would paint a nice big clear picture so I didn't have to guess. I hate guessing."

Sanders looked at me unsympathetically.

"Okay, I'll guess," I said. "The White House?"

Sanders nodded.

"Now I don't have any fucking proof about that," he said. "But when information like that goes up the ladder and nothing comes back down, that's usually where it's been stopped."

"Usually?," I asked. "Like this happens all the time?"

"What do you think, Brandt?" Sanders leaned his elbows against the table and lowered his voice. "All through the Eighties we were busting Pakistanis trying to smuggle nuclear material out of the country. But the administration would never accept that Pakistan was building the bomb. You see, there's a law that says the president has to notify Congress when he has knowledge of a country building nukes, so Congress can cut off aid to that country. But that's not what happened with Pakistan. Know why?"

"Because Pakistan was helping the U.S. arm the anti-Soviet rebels in Afghanistan."

Sanders nodded like a proud schoolmaster.

"So we let them get the bomb."

"We let them get the bomb," Sanders agreed. "You know, to be fucking honest, Brandt, sometimes I don't know what the taxpayers pay me for."

The Customs agent stared over my shoulder some more before continuing.

"Cutting to the chase, we got the bad guys and embarrassed Washington. The administration started stumbling all over itself trying to hide the fact it knew Iraq was building the bomb."

"And in the confusion, Hussein marched into Kuwait."

"And the rest is history," Sanders said smugly. "And now you know why they don't like me talking about the Iraqi case."

"But what does this have to do with Project Qari?"

"I have no fucking idea," Sanders said. "I was hoping you could tell me."

I fought the impulse to jump across the table and throttle the sucker but they still put people in prison for assaulting federal agents, even if you had justifiable cause. Sanders must have read my face.

"Before you get your fucking shorts in a knot, let me continue," he said. "When Washington was trying to block the investigation, we were copied on a lot of memorandums that went back and forth between State and Commerce. Now, understand, we weren't supposed to get these copies. Someone faxed them to us because they wanted us to know what was going on."

"You mean someone in Customs? In D.C.?"

"I don't know if anyone in Customs in D.C. could operate a fucking fax machine," Sanders said. "My guess was The Company."

"CIA?" Sanders nodded again. "Now who's playing James-fucking-Bond?"

The agent laughed. "I owe you that one," he said. "But I'm serious. CIA always gets tabs on these kinds of investigations."

"So what about the memos?"

"In all of them, there were references to a Project Qari. They were worried my investigation was jeopardizing it." Sanders shook his head. "We tried to find out what it was, but we got stonewalled each time."

"That's all you know?"

Sanders shrugged and stood. "It's pretty obvious Qari has something to do with the White House and Iraq, isn't it?" He held his hands out from his sides and bowed slightly. "Sorry I wasted your time. But . . ."

He looked past me again, a coy smile playing over his lips.

"Maybe that guy over there knows more."

Sanders nodded toward a man sitting two tables over. He was reading a newspaper held up high, hiding his face. When he lowered it, I recognized him immediately, even without the blue sun hat. He saw both of us looking at him, and the disgust that came to his face rivaled the disgust he showed the day he smashed into the old station wagon.

"Who is that son-of-a-bitch. He's been following me everywhere."

"I know," Sanders said. "I talked to him briefly when you were refilling our coffee."

"So who the hell is he?"

"He's our local liaison with the Mossad," Sanders said. "Israeli intelligence. Remember what I said about giving, Brandt. You let me know if he tells you anything, got it?"

Sanders walked away without waiting for an answer.

CHAPTER 18

He slowly folded his newspaper and laid it on the table, crossed his legs, and rested both hands on his knee. A tolerant smile played at his thin lips. "Hello, Mr. Brandt," he said. "You might as well sit."

"Sanders says you're with the Mossad."

A painful expression crossed his face. When it passed, he said, "Agent Sanders is a good investigator, but you may have noticed he likes to talk too much."

"You're with the Mossad," I said, answering my own question.

He only shrugged.

"My name is Tygard," he said. Despite his straw-colored hair, his eyes were a dark charcoal. His nose was prominent, aristocratic. He wore tan slacks and a tropical shirt that tugged at his belly. He waved a hand at a chair. "Please sit."

I pulled out a chair and sat, leaned across the table and eyed him warily, as if he might spook and run at any second. If he tried, I had every intention of leaping across the table and throttling him.

"You've been following me."

"Yes," he said. "Yes, I have."

"Why?"

"I need to talk with you."

"That's why you followed me?"

I heard my voice echo through the dining patio and saw people at other tables turn in our direction. Tygard closed his eyes with the same pained resignation. I lowered my voice and continued.

"You run a tag team on me just because you want to talk to me? You could have knocked on my door. Called me on the phone."

"A tag team?"

"I lost you in Mission Valley the other day. But I saw someone else picked me up later on. A tag team."

"I see." Tygard thought about that a moment, his thin lips pursed. He seemed perplexed. Then he shrugged and forgot about it. "I needed to know how much you knew," he finally said. "What you knew."

"About what?"

"About the death of Robert Stanning and about Project Qari." Tygard watched me for a moment. "You're frowning, Mr. Brandt."

"I was wondering why everyone wants to know what I know about Stanning and Qari," I said. "I'm the reporter. I'm the one who's supposed to ask the questions."

"I assure you, Mr. Brandt," Tygard said, "this is a barter arrangement. A trade. Even-steven, as you say."

"I give a little, you give a little," I said. "And, of course, I start the giving."

Tygard smiled and slapped the table. "That sounds like a wonderful way to begin."

So I began again. Telling him all I knew about Stanning and Qari, repeating it almost by rote now. When I finished, Tygard leaned back and pursed his lips.

"In other words," he said. "You know almost nothing, correct?"

I didn't seem to be impressing anyone. I was beginning to feel incompetent. "I've only been working on it a week."

The Mossad agent whistled softly for a while, thinking.

"This changes everything, I'm afraid," he said. "I had hoped I could simply be your Big Throat."

"Deep Throat," I corrected.

Tygard nodded. "Deep Throat, then. I expected just to confirm what you knew. But I see I need to be much more proactive than that."

"I'm terribly sorry to put you out," I growled.

"No need to be," he said, raising a hand and shaking his head. He leaned against the table and looked at me from under lidded eyes. "Tell me, Mr. Brandt. Just how much do you know about your country's policies toward Iraq?"

"Funny," I said. "It seems I was just having this conversation."

"Good. Then you understand how your country encouraged the sale of dangerous technology to that murderous madman Hussein?"

"It was widely reported by the press after the war," I said.

Tygard smiled smugly and turned his eyes toward heaven. I had the feeling he must have been a rabbi before becoming a spy.

"Widely reported, yes," he said, "but only after your president's precious popularity among the voters fell. Even then, what was disclosed only scraped the surface."

"Is this turning into a critique of the American press?"

"Not at all," Tygard said, still smiling. "I'm simply saying your press seemed reluctant to report what was happening while your president was riding his popularity wave. Later, they didn't seem to understand how deep it went, how much more to it there was."

"More?" I said. "What more?"

"There was Project Qari."

I said nothing. I simply looked at him and waited for him to explain. He looked back at me with that damn supercilious smile.

"Would you like to hear more about Project Qari?" he finally asked.

"Please," I said. I took out my notebook and pen, and held the pad in front of him. "Mind?"

"Please do," he said. "I may test you afterward."

I raised my eyebrows, what was left of them. He flicked his hand and shook his head.

"Oh, nothing," he said. "A little private joke. I used to be a schoolteacher. College professor, actually."

"That explains it," I mumbled.

"I'm sorry?"

"Nothing," I said. "Project Qari, please."

"Yes, very well then. Begin your note-taking," Tygard said. He cleared his throat. "To begin with, Project Qari was an off- the-books operation "

"A black project," I said, remembering what Sidney Clipper had told me.

Tygard shook his head.

"It was more than a black project, Mr. Brandt," he said. "Qari operated outside normal government channels. It was an off-the-books covert activity not unlike Operation Recovery."

"Operation Recovery?" I repeated. "What's that?"

"You probably know it better as Iran-Contra."

"Yes, you might say I know it very well."

"In fact, Recovery and Qari ran concurrently for some time," Tygard continued. "At the same time your White House was bartering missiles for hostages with Iran, it was also providing covert military assistance to Iraq.

"This, of course, was during the disastrous war between Iran and Iraq. Officially, the United States was neutral. But, in fact, your government was quite fearful that Iran might be victorious and spread its form of Islamic fundamentalism through the region. Not being able to accept this, your government set about to prop up Hussein's military forces. The most overt example of this, of course, was the naval convoy operation your country undertook to protect Kuwaiti oil tankers steaming through the Persian Gulf. Of course, everyone knew the crude oil in those tankers was Iraqi oil, not Kuwaiti. Helping Hussein export his oil helped him finance his war with Iran."

"This is hardly news," I said.

"Quite," Tygard said. "But your government's aid went far beyond that. Under Project Qari, the United States covertly provided Baghdad with a steady flow of weapons—bombs, guns, artillery. Also provided were military advisers, weapons technicians, even pilots to fly Iraq's few remaining operational jet fighters. All this done without the use of official American resources."

"And how was that?"

"Through secret contracts with your defense corporations and companies—contracts signed with Iraqi government but secretly paid for by your government," Tygard said. "They—the contractors—provided the materiel and the personnel, and none of it with any direct links to your government."

Tygard paused and waited for me to stop scribbling notes.

"You've heard of Dr. Gerald Bull?" he asked.

"Arms maker," I said. "An expert in long-range artillery. He designed that big cannon they found outside Baghdad. The Supergun."

"And a man with very close ties to your country's intelligence services. He was part of Qari until he was unfortunately shot outside his apartment in Brussels."

"Which most people believe was brought about by the Mossad."

Tygard flicked the accusation away with his hand.

"Not important," he said. "What *is* important, Mr. Brandt, is that Project Qari is still in effect."

CHAPTER 19

Y ou're saying my government is continuing to arm Iraq?"

I heard my own voice echoing through the dining patio again. Tygard's face showed that same pained expression of tolerant exasperation. He nodded slowly and deliberately.

"That's impossible," I said. I slammed the pen down. "The navy's enforcing an UN embargo against Baghdad. Nothing gets in or out. Hussein can't even sell his oil to raise money to buy arms."

"There is, however, a backdoor to Iraq—Jordan. It's been widely known for some time that Iraqi oil has been tankered through Jordan for sale," Tygard said. "Besides, Mr. Brandt, the desert is vast. There are uncountable numbers of ancient caravan routes known only to Bedouin traders who, for the proper number of dinars, will transport people or merchandise without questions."

The teacher in Tygard emerged again. The Mossad agent couldn't resist giving a history lesson. He pointed to the notepad and pen before continuing.

"Please, start taking notes again," he said. "I really may test you on this."

MARTIN ROY HILL

He smiled and planted his elbows on the table, his chin resting on his clasped hands.

"When the war between Iran and Iraq ended with a negotiated cease fire, Baghdad was in a quandary," he began. "Hussein's oil facilities were shattered by bombing, his army was war weary, and its equipment worn. To make matters worse, he had rebellious Kurds along both his northern and southern borders. Hussein needed to rebuild his army and he was determined to build it bigger and stronger than before.

"Project Qari should have ended with the cease fire between the two belligerents. But the companies contracted for Project Qari saw what you might call a maturing market in Iraq, and they were not willing to leave it behind. You have to remember, Mr. Brandt, at this point in time, the Cold War was winding down and there was talk among your politicians of defense cuts and a peace dividend. Companies like General Technologies and ConEl were faced with having their lifeblood cut off. And these companies sought financial salvation in Hussein's military buildup.

"With help from Baghdad, the companies involved in Qari were able to convince your White House to keep the operation going. To be honest, your White House didn't take much convincing. First, it was still fearful of Iran's religious expansionism. But also, your government was faced with a massive trade deficit. It decided not only to continue Project Qari's clandestine activities, but to expand on them. It actually began encouraging American companies to do business openly with Baghdad, including selling Hussein so-called dual use technologies."

I stopped scribbling. "Dual use?"

Tygard nodded. "Technology can be used for either peaceful purposes or military purposes." The Mossad agent glanced at the sky for inspiration, found it and gave me an example. "For instance, a computer system was sold to Baghdad ostensibly for designing new oil drilling equipment. Instead, it ended up in a military laboratory where it was used to design parts for a ballistic missile. Do you see what I mean by dual use?"

I nodded my understanding and he went on.

"Of course the United States was not alone in this. Britain, France, Germany, and others were all encouraging their companies to go after the Iraqi dinar." Tygard smiled and leaned forward, and spoke *sotto voce*. "And they say we Jews are greedy? You have not seen greed, my friend, until you've seen a German businessman smell money. Oh, yes, and they can smell it." He tapped his nose with a finger. "They've got the nose for it."

Tygard leaned back and chuckled with satisfaction. He took a deep breath and stretched luxuriously. When he finished, he resumed his professorial air.

"The irony, of course," he said, "was that Baghdad was bankrupt. Iranian bombers had devastated its oil facilities. Iraq had plenty of oil, but it was stuck in the ground and there was no way of getting it out. Baghdad devised a means of financing its military buildup with a series of loans from your country as well as the others. It would use the money from one loan to pay off the other loans, with each loan being larger than the last."

"A Ponzi scheme," I said.

"I beg your pardon?"

"A Ponzi scheme. Also known as a pyramid scam. You get people to invest in a phony investment concern and pay dividends to the first investors with the money from newer investors. All along you skim off the top."

"I like that," Tygard said. "A pyramid scam. Quite appropriate, don't you think?"

"I think we need to cut to the chase, Tygard," I said. "We're getting into history here. This is all old news."

"Quite," Tygard said. "Let's cut to the chase." He placed his hand on the table and adjusted his shoulders. "Project Qari continued in operation up until the time your current president drew his famous line in the sand. Then, and only then, did he begin to doubt the wisdom of continuing to supply arms to Baghdad. Considering your military forces were about to go to war with Hussein's, I suspect your president felt a little like he was aiding and abetting the enemy."

Tygard seemed pleased with his bit of wit. His smile reeked of smugness and his eyes fluttered superciliously. I couldn't help but smash his smugness.

"Yes," I said. "Sort of like the way your country sells arms—including nuclear weapons technology—to the neo-fascist apartheid government of South Africa."

The smug smile vanished, replaced nearly instantly by another, this one more bemused.

"Touché, Mr. Brandt," he said. "Geo-politics and strange bedfellows—none of us are immune, I fear. Nevertheless..." His index finger sprang to attention. "The point is Project Qari foolishly continued. Many of Hussein's so-called 'guest-ages' were technicians and weapons experts providing military assistance to the Iraqi military through Project Qari."

A couple and their two small children rose from the table next to ours. She was young and plump, someone who took to heart the tales of pregnant women's eating habits. The children were equally plump. The father was young and muscled and wore his hair in Marine high-and-tight fashion. He wore a Desert Storm T-shirt. Everyone in town that year was wearing them, it seemed. As they passed, the Marine's stare cut through us like cold steel. The two kids yelped as their mother pulled them away from us as if we were child molesters.

"Oh, dear," Tygard said. "I believe they overheard us."

"So they'll have nightmares tonight," I said. "You said Qari stopped. But earlier you said it was still in operation."

Tygard steepled his fingertips. "Stop, it did. But not for long."

The Mossad agent broke the steeple in half and looked absently at his fingers. "Would you like some coffee, Mr. Brandt?"

"No. What do you mean not for long?"

"I would love some coffee. Would you excuse me?"

Tygard started to rise from his chair but I grabbed his arm and pulled him back down.

"Stop playing with me, Tygard."

"Mr. Brandt, I assure you I am not playing with you," he said. "I truly want some coffee."

Without looking around, I knew people were watching us. I could feel their eyes looking at us. The dark pits of Tygard's eyes warily scanned the tables. I let go and with a pleasant nod, he left the table. To my surprise, he returned a few minutes later with a steaming cup of coffee and cream.

"Now, where was I?" he said.

"But not for long."

"Right." Tygard scanned the open dining area again and his eyes looked worried. "Do you mind if we walk? I believe we've attracted the attention of the other diners with our last display."

"Don't worry about it," I told him. "They'll just believe we're two gay lovers having a tiff."

"If it's all the same, Mr. Brandt, I'd rather walk." Tygard stood, slipped on dark glasses and gestured toward the escalator leading to the upper decks. "Frankly, I don't relish the idea of kissing you goodbye to carry on the scenario. Shall we?"

We took the moving staircase up two floors and got off. Tygard led the way past the expensive department stores, the smaller but equally expensive boutiques, and the fastfood outlets. The walkways were crowded with holiday shoppers, though nowhere near as crowded as they had been in earlier years. A boy about six rushed past carrying a mustard-smeared hotdog on a stick. He careened off Tygard, who grabbed the child and set him back on course without spilling a drop of his coffee. The child sped off only to rush into another shopper. His treat fell to the ground with a splat, and he began to cry.

"Where was I again?" Tygard asked.

"But not for long."

"Yes." The Mossad agent sipped his coffee. "Shortly after the air war began in Desert Storm, it became obvious to your country that Hussein's military was being decimated by the Coalition's air superiority. Certain people in Washington began worrying that a militarily weakened Iraq would open the door to Iranian expansionism—exactly what Washington had hoped to stem by building up Baghdad's armed forces."

"So the White House pulled the stop order on Qari?" I was trying to scribble notes and walk without bumping into every pedestrian in the mall. In the back of my mind, I worried I wouldn't be able to read my notes later on.

"Precisely," Tygard said. "Project Qari was reinstated even though there was a UN embargo against Iraq. The back door was Jordan, which remained allied with Baghdad."

I stopped walking and lowered the notepad. Tygard stopped a few paces ahead and looked at me quizzically.

"Look, I can't believe what you're telling me, Tygard," I said.

"No?"

"You expect me to believe the White House began arming a country it was at war with?"

"It's not that unusual, Mr. Brandt," he said. "History is replete with such examples. I know. I was a history professor." Tygard stepped closer and touched my arm to move me out of the way of the traffic flow. "For instance, your country provided Japan much of the steel it needed to build its navy and the oil it needed to run that navy, even though it was well known in your government for at least a decade that the United States and Japan were headed toward hostilities.

"It was worse with Germany. Many people realized as early as the end of World War I there would be another war with Germany. Still, that didn't stop American companies from helping build the Nazi war machine. Then there were the American oil companies that sold petroleum to Nazi Germany even as your country's troops were attempting to liberate Europe. And—"

"And your country's relationship with South Africa."

"Quite."

Tygard waited for a group of shoppers to pass by before continuing. He moved closer to me, lowered his voice, and positioned himself against the wall so he could watch the passers-by.

"You're familiar with the October Surprise?" he asked.

"Of course," I said, nodding. "There were allegations that Ronald Reagan's campaign staff held secret negotiations with Iran to convince the Ayatollah Khomeini not to release the embassy hostages before 1980 presidential elections. Reagan's people were afraid President Carter's negotiators would succeed in getting the hostages freed—what they called an October Surprise—and swing the election in Carter's favor."

"Precisely."

"I also know a congressional investigation didn't find any hard evidence of such a conspiracy."

"Of course, they didn't!" Tygard's smile and voice led me to believe he knew otherwise. "What you're probably not aware of, Mr. Brandt, is that in 1968 your President Johnson was close to negotiating a peace settlement between North and South Vietnam. Unfortunately, Mr. Nixon's campaign staff held secret talks with the Saigon government and convinced them to pull out of the peace negotiations. I'm afraid Mr. Nixon also feared an October Surprise."

I stared at Tygard and thought of my dead brother. If what Tygard said was true, it meant the Vietnam War needlessly continued for seven more years at the costs of tens of thousands of American lives. I didn't want to believe the Mossad agent, but my knowledge of what people seeking or holding power will do attain it and keep it forced me to concede its probability. Tygard beckoned me to continue walking.

"The point is, Mr. Brandt, the White House did not want Hussein's army destroyed. Their view of that madman had not changed. He's a devil, but he's your devil."

"And better the devil you know."

"Precisely," Tygard said, resurrecting the pious smile. "And that is the reason your president called a cease-fire and prevented General Schwarzkoff from marching all the way to Baghdad. But mark my word, Mr. Brandt, if Qari continues, there will be another American war with Iraq—and sooner rather than later."

I thought about what Tygard said, and in my mind's eye, I saw the slaughter on the Highway of Death. Another war with Iraq could only be worse, and might not be as easy to finish as Desert Storm.

"How did Stanning fit into this?" I finally asked.

"Robert Stanning was ConEl's liaison with the Iraqis—what you might call their front man. It was his responsibility to set up a network of false companies in Europe and the Mid-East that ConEl used as its end-users for trans-shipping its materials to Baghdad. Those companies also provided ConEl an employment front for the technicians it provided Hussein."

It was as if someone opened a curtain and let light into the dark closet where I keep my brain. Everything began clicking into place.

"That's why ConEl maintains Stanning no longer worked for them," I said. "In effect, he was working for the front companies."

"Exactly," Tygard exclaimed with the excitement of a proud teacher. "When Qari was deactivated, Stanning was sent to Europe to close down his network of companies. However, when the White House rescinded the deactivation order, he suddenly found himself back in Iraq trying to reestablish his contacts. Unfortunately for

Mr. Stanning, he was caught in one of your bombing attacks."

"Actually, he was caught twice by friendly fire," I murmured. "Not a lucky man."

"Most unlucky," Tygard agreed.

"Do you know of a man named Roger Sherman?"

Tygard enjoyed a short, caustic laugh.

"Oh, indeed I do," he said. "Most people in my line of work have heard of Colonel Sherman."

"What was his role in Qari?"

"Why, Mr. Brandt," Tygard said with mock surprise. "I thought you knew. Colonel Sherman is the secret operations officer overseeing Project Qari."

"He runs Qari? Still?"

"Yes, indeed. Ah, here we are!"

The Mossad agent stopped in front of a Mrs. Fields cookie shop and browsed the window display.

"Why are you telling me this?" I asked.

Tygard beckoned me to follow him inside. "I really can't resist these."

He ordered a dozen of the chocolate chip goodies, and wolfed one down before we'd even left the shop. I declined his offer of a cookie, which I considered a fine example of self-control.

"Why are you talking to me, Tygard?"

"I learned through an informant that you were looking into Mrs. Stanning's lawsuit," he said, licking melted chocolate off his fingers. "You have to understand, there is nothing more my country would like than to have the truth known about Mr. Stanning, ConEl, and Project Qari exposed. You can understand why we don't feel comfortable with your country providing arms and assistance to Baghdad. That Supergun of Dr. Bull's was pointed at Tel Aviv, Mr. Brandt, not Tehran."

"You want to stop Qari."

Tygard nodded. "We want to stop Qari. What kind of fruit are you?"

We had stopped at the entrance to the parking garage.

"Banana," I said.

"Pity. I'm a grape. Or was it cherry?"

"Did you know someone tried to kill Thomas Hess?"

"I read about it in the paper," Tygard said. He continued smiling benignly. "Terrible."

"Another ConEl official, Jack Sweeney, also died recently," I said. "Did you know that?"

"I believe I read that, too, in the paper. Suicide wasn't it?"

"The police believe he may have been thrown off that roof."

"How interesting," Tygard said. "Crime is rampant in this city."

"Listen, Tygard," I said. "A little advice. I don't think the American government would look too kindly on the Mossad if it decided to do to our defense industry leaders what it did to Gerry Bull."

"Mr. Brandt!"

"And it could backfire. In fact, it may already have." Tygard looked at me with what I could only describe as mild interest. "Sweeney was getting ready to talk about Qari when he was killed."

Tygard took a deep breath and smiled tolerantly.

"Mr. Brandt," he said. "My country is most interested in making this information public—if not by you, then by someone else. We are hardly motivated to silence people about this."

He reached into his pocket and handed me a business card for an import-export company.

"You may contact me at this office if you need to," Tygard said. "And Mr. Brandt? A little advice for you, too. I am a lone player. I do not have an organization here. If someone was running what you call a tag team on you, it was not the Mossad."

Tygard started walking toward the parking garage but stopped and turned back. He waited for two young women to pass. "But you should know this, Mr. Brandt," he finally said. "Anything Colonel Sherman is involved with is a very dangerous game, indeed. I would walk very carefully if I were you."

He turned and disappeared into the shadows of the garage.

CHAPTER 20

Jo spent the night, but we didn't make love. There were too many emotions surging through both of us to make room for tenderness or lust. More than anything else, anger brimmed within us, and we took it out on each other.

It started when I explained what Tygard, the Mossad agent, had told me. I paced the floor, drink in hand, too excited to sit, and too excited to see the color drain from Jo's face or hear the stony silence that enveloped her. When I finished, she sat perfectly still on the couch, her eyes focused on something I couldn't see.

"I can't believe it," she said slowly.

"Believe it," I said, jabbing a finger at her. "I've seen this too many times. During Iran-Contra, the government used to let cargo planes carrying drugs land and off-load at Air Force bases as payment for flying supplies to the Contras. I've seen it all before, Jo. I believe it."

"It doesn't shock you?"

She was dressed in civvies, tight jeans, and a white blouse like the one she wore that night at the Launch Pad. Her face was hard, her voice harder.

"Shock me?" I said. "Of course, it shocks me."

"Does it, Peter? You seem very excited about it."

"Of course, I'm excited." I paced around the room filled with that excitement, not comprehending what Jo was after. "This is a great story. This story is going to blow the socks off people all the way to Washington. This is the kind of story we live for."

"We?"

"We." Now I jabbed my finger at myself. "Reporters. Journalists"

Jo looked at me. Her eyes held the cool bite of an Arctic night.

"That's all this is to you, isn't it?" she said. "A story. Your name on a piece of paper." The iciness in her eyes and voice froze me where I stood. I finally began to understand, but it was too late.

"I'm sorry," I said.

"Sorry?" Jo slammed her drink on the light stand and stood abruptly, wincing at the pain it caused. "Sorry? Do you understand what this means?" I nodded. "Do you really, Peter Brandt?"

She limped to the window and stood there in silence. I went to her, but she pulled away from me.

"People died over there, Peter," she finally said. The ice was gone from her voice now. It was low and soft, barely above a whisper. "A lot more were hurt. People I knew, people I cared for. People I was responsible for. And all the goddamn parades they throw over here aren't going to bring them back. And now you tell me it was all an insidious joke?"

"I know, damn it." I heard the edgy hardness in my own voice. "That's why this story's important. People should know "

"No, you don't know!" she screamed. "You've never had people you were responsible for get killed. You don't know what it's like."

She was wrong. I knew precisely what it was like. But I didn't bring it up now.

Jo took a step toward her drink, and her bad leg gave slightly. She caught herself and pounded her hip with her fist.

"Damn it, damn it, damn it!" I grabbed her fist, but she wrestled it away. "Look at me, Peter. This is what it's about. I'm never going to walk right again. I'm never going to—" Her sobs caught up with her. She wiped a mascara-stained tear from her eye. "I'm never going to be pretty again."

She sat on the couch, head held in her hands. Laughter began mixing with her sobs.

"Pretty again? Talk about getting your priorities straight." She looked up. Her eyes were red, her face stained with runny makeup. She shook her head. "I'm sorry, Peter."

I sat beside her and put my arm around her. This time she didn't break away.

"No, I'm sorry," I said. "You're right. I wasn't thinking right."

She lifted her head to me and let me kiss her.

"We're just two of the sorriest people on earth," she said.

Later, we lay in bed together, her hips planted against mine, my arms encircling her. I drifted asleep to the sound of her sobs. When I woke in the morning, her pillow was still wet from her tears.

§

The phone was ringing when I stepped from the shower. Jo had left early, dressing in the dark and softly kissing me goodbye. She promised everything was okay between us, but I still had a sick, empty feeling in my gut. The phone irritated me. I let the machine answer it.

"Brandt, you son-of-a-bitch!" It was Sidney Clipper's voice and it was not pleasant. "What the hell you think you're doing to me, you goddamn motherfu—"

I grabbed the phone handset and said, "Sidney, what's wrong?"

I didn't need to hold the phone to my ear. In fact, I could almost hear Sidney without the phone.

"There you are, you asshole," he growled.

"What are you so damn upset about?"

"Upset? Upset? Why the hell shouldn't I be upset after what you did?"

"What are you talking about, Sid?"

"I'm talking about sticking the goddamn feds on me, that's what asshole." Sidney was shrieking now. He was out of control and I considered hanging up. Something kept me listening. "You betrayed me. You put them on to me. They took my guidance system, for Christ's sake."

"Sid, calm down. Calm the hell down." I wasn't awake enough to follow everything he was saying. I wasn't sure his ranting was worth following. "Tell me what happened."

"Don't tell me to calm down, you son-of-a-bitch! I'll tell you what happened. They came this morning. The goddamn feds. You put them on to me, don't deny it."

"What feds, Sidney?" He wasn't listening. The phone line was filled with vindictiveness and malevolence. Sidney seemed certain I was the devil incarnate. The morning takeoffs from Lindbergh began screaming overhead. I shouted to overcome the noise on the line and the noise in the air. "Hold on, Sid. Let me get dressed and I'll be right over."

I pulled on a pair of jeans and a brown T-shirt, slipped my old khaki bush jacket over that, and gunned the Mustang out of the court and toward the freeway. I didn't see Tygard behind me. If anyone else was following me, I couldn't tell. I goosed the six-cylinders through Mission Valley to the I-15 and turned north to Tierrasanta.

Sidney was a mess. He was wearing baggy shorts that looked like they were last washed before his divorce. His flabby belly hung loosely over the edge of the shorts, peeking out from the bottom of a stained white T-shirt with a faded beer ad on it. His thin, sandy hair stood out in all directions, as if he slept with one toe in an electric socket. The horn-rims sat crooked on his nose, making his eyes appear as if Picasso had painted them.

The apartment was a reflection of its inhabitant. In the center of the room, the mattress sat cockeyed on its bedsprings, the bedclothes balled up on top of it. The two paintings were ripped from the wall and left on the floor. The pinups were on the floor, too, balled up like the sheets and blankets. There were dirty dishes in the sink. One dish had been dropped face down on the floor and stepped on, the spoiled food ground into the carpet.

Sidney was calmer but sullen. He let me in without a word, then sat on the bed and glared at me with angry, reddened eyes. He smelled like stale beer and puke.

"Like what your friends did, Brandt?"

"Snap out of it, Sidney," I said sharply. "Just tell me what happened."

The sting in my voice seemed to shoot through Sidney's self-pity. He pursed his lips, straightened himself, and ran a hand through his mop. His swollen eyes stared dully at me.

"Godzilla and King Kong came to the door and said they were federal agents," he said. "Next thing I knew I was lying on the floor and they were acting like this was Tokyo."

"They who, Sidney?" I tried to moderate my voice but I was getting tired of Sidney's round-robin answers.

"I told you. Godzilla and King Kong," he said. I returned his stare. Finally, his shoulders moved in a shrug. "I don't know. Two big guys, short hair, dark glasses. They said they were federal agents."

"They show you ID?"

Sidney shook his head.

"Did you ask?"

"For Christ's sake, Brandt. When the feds poke their noses in your door, you don't ask for their autograph. They had those funny little earphones in their ears and bulges under their arms that weren't muscles."

"How were they dressed?"

Sidney closed his eyes and shook his head. The gesture seemed to pain him. "I don't know, Brandt. Blue jeans. No, one had jeans, the other was wearing some kind of dark slacks. Those light-weight jackets cops wear, like you see on TV."

"Raid jackets?" Sidney nodded. "What'd it say on the jackets?"

"Nothing," Sidney said, shaking his head.

What good was a raid jacket that didn't identify you as a cop or federal agent? I didn't think Sidney would understand the question nor have the answer, so I didn't ask him.

"Okay," I said. "Tell me what they did."

Sidney waved his arms around the room. His eyes grew large as his voice rose.

"Take a look, Brandt, for Christ's sake. They pushed me around and tore the place up. They took my guidance system."

"What did they say?"

"They said they knew I was talking to you, that I was jeopardizing national security, and if I knew what was good for me I'd shut up." Sidney looked at the blank spot above the TV where his deadly montage had hung. "They said they were taking my guidance system as evidence. Said they might come back and arrest me for government theft, maybe even espionage."

"Did they name me? Did they use my name"

"Of course," Sidney snapped. "How else would I know you set me up?"

"Sid, think about it. Why would I set you up?"

Sidney thought about it. After a while, his shoulders lifted and dropped. "I don't know."

"Someone's been following me," I told Sid. "I thought I lost them when I came here the other day. I guess I didn't. I'm sorry."

Sidney stood and slid the glasses back up his nose. "Christ," he hissed, pronouncing it as two syllables. "Thanks, Brandt. Thanks a whole fucking lot."

He shuffled toward the bathroom, hacked a load of phlegm into the toilet, then took a beer from the refrigerator and chugged half of it by the time he crossed back to the bed. Without thinking, I glanced at my watch and shook my head.

"This is just what I need," Sidney moaned. He was sitting on the bed, his head hanging over his knees, the beer grasped tightly in both hands. "Just what I need."

"It'll work out, Sid," I said.

"Oh, yeah, sure. First, I lose my job, then my family. Everybody in the fucking world is slapping me around. How can I beat those odds, Brandt?"

"Come off it, Sid." I could hear the tightness in my voice. I was getting sick of Sidney's self-pity. "You're a highly trained engineer. You can get a job, start over—"

"Doing what?" Sidney shouted. "Designing boilers? I'm a weapons man, Brandt. What do I know about boilers?"

"You can adapt, Sid," I said. "We all have to."

"Christ, Brandt, you just don't understand, do you?" Sidney was breathing hard now, his voice unsteady. "The cards are stacked against me. I'm too old. I got experience, talent, brains . . . and years. No one wants to pay for the years part of the equation anymore. I'm being tossed out like a goddamn used refrigerator. They plan it that way."

"They?"

"Them! All of them!" Sidney was on his feet, screaming again. His face was the same crimson as his eyes. The veins in his neck stood out like mountain ridges. "The Hesses, my wife, those guys this morning. For all I know you, too, Brandt. They all stack it against me. How can a guy like me ever win?"

I've never been comfortable in the presence of madness, and the way Sidney was crushing his beer can was making me feel mightily uncomfortable. The beer frothed up and flowed over his hand onto the carpet. Sidney didn't seem to notice. He stared at me, then closed his eyes and threw himself on the bed, sobbing.

I went out the glass door and started up the Mustang. I drove back to the beach with the windows all open, breathing the air and wishing I had a cigarette to burn away the taste left in my mouth.

CHAPTER 21

My stomach growled like a wildcat by the time I reached Ocean Beach. I bypassed my street and turned down Newport Avenue, OB's tiny, two-lane main street cluttered with second-hand shops, darkened bars, and cheap restaurants specializing in good and abundant food. Presiding over the rest was the Newport Cinema, a grand old dame of a movie house, the kind you don't see anymore, with one large screen, balcony seats, and prices a family of four could actually afford. She'd seen good times and bad, the cinema, with her superannuated marquee announcing through the years the showing of popular films, porn flicks, and now artsy movies with foreign titles. She was showing one now, but there were so many letters missing from the marquee I couldn't figure out which one.

The morning marine layer was beginning to burn off. The air was sweet and salty with ocean brine. Old folks shuffled along on their morning constitutionals, passed up by blond youths in wet suits lugging their surfboards to the beach. Now and then someone in tie-dyed T-shirts and tattered jeans, and sporting long greasy hair sauntered by, artifacts of the days when Ocean Beach was

San Diego's hippie colony. That was a long time ago, and most of the love children from those days had grown up, cleaned up, registered Republican, voted Ronald Reagan into office, and did their best to become the next Donald and Ivana Trump. Michael Larrs was one of those, and I tried not to remember that as I parked in front of Margarita's Mexican restaurant for fear it would dull my appetite.

I ordered *machaca con huevoes* with flour tortillas, refried beans and black coffee, and after a moment of nostalgic reverie over similar meals in faraway places, I tried to sort out Sidney Clipper's rantings.

Sidney's description of the intruders didn't make sense. Feds typically wouldn't wear raid jackets to question someone and, if they did, the jackets would clearly identify them as FBI, DEA or whatever in bright, bold letters. Two possibilities entered my mind as I wolfed down the spiced eggs and shredded beef. Godzilla and King Kong, as Sid called them, might have been rent- a-cops from ConEl's security force sent to scare him into silence. If that were true, Jo Rice, as security liaison, may have been involved in rousting Sid. I didn't care for that option.

The other possibility was the one suggested by Mike McCarty: that the intruders, like the people following me, were part of some extra-legal federal agency—not the feebes or drug enforcement, but the kind that doesn't normally carry ID or badges. I didn't care much for that option, either.

The answer was waiting for me when I got home.

The message light was blinking on the answering machine. It was Tom Collier at the magazine, asking me to call him immediately. Something in his voice made my breakfast turn sour. I grabbed the phone and dialed his number.

"Pete," Collier said without any other greeting, "I don't know what you've been doing but you got me into hot water, for sure. I'm feeling like a lobster whose days are numbered."

"Wh-what's happening, Tom?"

There was silence on the other end, then a sigh. "I gotta kill the Stanning assignment," he said.

"What?"

"Hey, it's not my idea, Pete. You know how I feel about this story "

"Yeah, you were hoping to get laid."

"Well, yeah." I could picture him shrugging. "So you understand how important it was to me. But I've got my orders. The story's dead."

"Why, Tom?" My hand tightened on the receiver. My voice was growing just as tight. "You going to tell me why?"

Another silence. Another sigh. Tom lowered his voice to a harsh whisper.

"The publisher called me into his office first thing this morning," he said. "There were two federal agents there "

"Federal agents?"

"That's what I said, right?"

"What'd they look like?"

"I don't know," Tom said. "Dick Tracy and Elliott Ness."

"Describe them, Tom. What were they wearing?"

Tom stammered for a while, trying to collect his thoughts. I had as much trust in Tom's ability to recognize a genuine fed as I did in Sidney Clipper's.

"Two guys, one average height but stocky," he said. "Not fat, just big. The other was tall and big. Clean cut. Business suits. They looked and talked like attorneys, but they each had those funny little earplugs in their ears."

Not the same two who visited Sidney Clipper, I thought.

"Where were they from?"

"From?" Tom said. "The government, Sherlock. Where else?"

"Tom, what fucking agency did they say they were from?"

Tom fumbled over his thoughts again. I got the feeling he wasn't quite up to answering these questions.

"The publisher just said they were from the government," he finally said. "I figured they were FBI or CIA or something."

"Or something," I murmured.

"What?"

"Nothing," I said. "What did they say?"

"They said you were stepping all over a matter of national security and they wanted us to pull you off," Tom said. "The publisher didn't believe that and told them so. Then they got mean."

Tom lowered his voice even more. I wished he'd simply get up and close his office door, but I knew he never did that. With the door closed, he couldn't watch the office women walk by.

"They threatened to confiscate the whole issue, and let the courts decide whether it was legal," he continued. "The publisher said he could survive that. Then they pulled out the big threat. They said if we published the piece, the IRS would be on us like maggots on a road kill. That did it. End of story. *Fini*. But don't think I'm screwing you over on this, Pete. We had a contract on this, and I'm honoring it. I'm mailing you a $1,000 kill fee, okay?"

"We agreed on three grand for the fee, Tom," I snapped. "That contract stipulates a 50 percent kill fee. That's fifteen hundred, not a thousand."

"Oh, yeah, that's right," Tom said. I could hear the disappointment in his voice. "You know how bad my math is, Pete. Fifteen hundred, okay?"

"Yeah, sure," I said. I heard the frustration in my own voice. The line went silent for a moment, then I worked some sarcasm into my words to replace the disappointment.

"Hey, Tom," I said. "Guess the real tragedy in all this is how it screws up your chances with the Stanning widow, huh?"

"My heart is broken, Pete," he said, his sorrow unconvincing. "She was the love of my life."

Then the line went dead.

§

The desktop made a cracking noise as I slammed my fist down on it. I sat staring at it, expecting it to split in two. It stayed upright. I seethed inside. My breathing was hard and angry. I raised my fist to see if I could take the desk down in two blows when the phone rang.

It was Jo, spitting with rage.

"I just got a nasty little visit," she said.

"Don't tell me. A couple of federal agents, right?"

"Just one, from CID," Jo said. "How'd you know?"

"CID?" I raced through my mental dictionary of military acronyms. "Criminal Investigative Division? He said he was with the army CID?"

"Yeah, that's what he said," Jo answered. "I'm not sure I believe him, though. Little prick. He wanted to know what I was doing hanging around a reporter. He said I was endangering national security. He knew about me trying to access the Qari files on the computer and asking questions around here about it."

"What do you mean you're not sure he was CID? Did he show you any ID?"

"Of course," Jo said. "I made him. But you can buy stuff like that in mail order catalogues these days. I got the feeling he was CIA. Pete, do you know something about this?"

"I think so," I said. "First, tell me what he said."

"He wanted me to stop asking about Qari. National security, he said. And he wanted me to stop talking to you. He said talking to you could ruin my army career."

Jo laughed lightly before continuing. Hearing her laugh gave me a strange, warm feeling despite what we were discussing.

"I told the son-of-a-bitch my career was probably already over because of my wound. Then he turned around and threatened me with a bad discharge. At that point, I invited him out of my office with a few well-chosen four-letter words."

"Good for you, Jo."

"Peter, are you going to tell me what's going on?"

So I told her, describing how Sidney Clipper was roughed up and how the magazine was threatened with a tax audit and killed my assignment. When I finished, the line was silent. When Jo finally spoke, her voice was low and distant. She almost sounded frightened.

"What are you going to do now, Peter?" she asked. "You're not dropping this, are you?"

She made it sound like dropping the story was tantamount to dropping her. And from somewhere deep inside of me, I knew I wasn't going to do that. I knew I couldn't.

"I'll just look for someone else to sell it to," I said. My voice trembled, and I cleared my throat before continuing. "I don't know just who yet, but someone. It's a good story."

"It's a good story," Jo repeated sadly. "I'll see you tonight?"

"Sure."

"Good," Jo said. The line was silent again and I figured it was about time to hang up when Jo remembered something. "Oh, I did some checking on Roger Sherman, about what your Israeli friend told you."

"Yeah?"

"Before Sherman retired, he was assigned to ConEl as project officer for CCOMS," she said. "That just meant he oversaw the implementation of the contract. What's curious though is that ConEl hired him after he retired. Now that used to be done a lot, but Congress passed a law in the Eighties prohibiting it."

"The revolving door law," I said, remembering something Sidney Clipper told me.

"Yeah, but no one raised a stink about it. Strange, huh?"

"Strange," I said.

We made plans to meet at my place that evening, then she hung up. I stared out the window trying to figure what to do next. The sun had taken over the sky now, and it shined yellow through the trees. The momma bird and her chick were back. I watched her feed her youngling until a jet thundered overhead and sent both mother and child flittering through the branches. I finally picked up the phone and dialed the number for the Los Angeles bureau of the newsweekly I worked for sometimes.

"Pete, how are you doing?" Marsha Hand, the bureau chief, spoke with the same New York inflection as Special Agent Sanders. "Listen, New York loved your last file."

"Great," I said. "I think I have something they should love even more."

I synopsized the Qari story for her, providing just enough detail to entice but not enough to let them follow up on their own. Michael Larrs wasn't the only journalist I didn't trust.

"That sounds hot, Peter," Marsha said. "You're sure of your information?" I told her I was. "Then let me call New York and see what they say. I'll get right back to you."

I put an Eagles tape on the stereo and played it softly while I made coffee and waited for Marsha to call back. When the phone finally rang, I heard a New York accent on the other end, but it wasn't Marsha Hand.

"Brandt, Sanders. Had any visitors lately?"

I slumped in the chair behind the desk and sighed. "You, too?"

"Oh, you have been visited?"

"Not me," I said. "But everyone I know seems to. What happened?"

"A couple stiffs with dark glasses and radios stuck in their ears took me in with my agent in charge and read us the riot act."

"Did they say who they were with?"

"No."

"So?"

"Not feebies," Sanders said. "No one legit, in my opinion. But all I can say is they were the type of guys who don't have official personnel files. I'm really beginning to wonder if I'm on the right side."

"What did they say?"

"Bastards knew I met you at the deli," Sander said. "They must've been tailing you. Did you know that?"

"I had suspicions," I said. "What did they tell you, Sanders? Short version."

"Short order? I don't talk to you anymore."

"You're talking to me now."

"Fuck them. And I told them that." Sanders lowered his voice. "I just wanted to warn you, let you know what was happening. You know our friend from Tel Aviv?"

"Tygard?"

"Yeah. Well, they must have seen him talking to you, too. He called me this morning. Seems he's been declared *persona non grata*. He's got a week to leave the country. Just thought you should know what's going down."

I thanked Sanders, and meant it. The line beeped; my call-waiting telling me another call was trying to ring through. I wondered who else could be calling me to say they had had a visit. I let it beep.

"Is it safe talking to me?" I asked. "They might have your phone tapped."

"Like I said Brandt, fuck them." Sanders chuckled. Even his laugh had an accent. "Besides, I'm calling from a phone booth uptown. Don't let the fuckers get you down."

CHAPTER 22

I pressed the phone button and answered the call on hold. It was a telephone solicitor again, offering me subscriptions I didn't need. The Texas drawl was slow and casual.

Locking up the bungalow, I walked down to the beach, found a pay phone I hadn't used recently, and dialed Fred Danbury's number. I asked for Fred, but the woman who answered the phone said he was out of the office.

"I'm sorry," I said, "but Fred just called me, wanted me to call him back. The name's Brandt. Peter Brandt."

"I'm sorry, Mr. Brandt," the woman said. "But Fred left this morning and said he wouldn't be back until late this afternoon. I assure you; if he were here, I would put you through. This office is not in the habit of putting people off. It's not good business, you know."

I apologized and hung up. I stared at the phone, not certain what had happened. Were the persons harassing Sidney Clipper, Jo, Sanders, and Tygard now beginning to play with my own mind? Did they somehow imitate Fred's voice to make a fool of me? Or, perhaps, to let me know they knew who my most intimate source was? Or was the call from a genuine telemarketer who simply sounded like the ex-CIA pilot?

Maybe I was just going crazy from the stress.

Then I turned and saw a mountain of a man leaning against the small wall that separated the beach from the boardwalk. He was watching me while gray smoke swirled around him from his usual little cigar. His salt-and-pepper moustache stretched across his face in a grin.

"Hey, Pete! *Como esta?*"

"I thought you just called me?"

"I did." Fred pulled a flip-top cellular phone out of his pocket and held it up proudly, shaking his head with wonder. "Y'know, all those years with The Company and we never had anything like these here things."

"You called me on that?"

"Yep."

"From here?"

Fred shook his head. "Nope. From across the street of your place. Then I followed you here. Y'know, son, you really ought to be more cognizant of your surroundings, hear?"

"Fred, what the hell are you doing here?"

Fred was dressed in dark slacks, alligator cowboy boots, and a light blue pullover polo shirt that stretched across his round gut. His hair was thick and dusty with gray, and his closely cropped moustache ended in points aimed sharply downward. He always reminded me of an older Stacy Keach.

He watched a young beauty in a low-slung bikini pass, smiled at her with his teeth showing, the cigar sticking straight out like a phallus. The girl passed without seeming to notice either of us. Then he turned to me.

"You got your ass in a sling, partner," he said, motioning me to walk. "I feel responsible."

"Responsible? How?"

"I got a call last night from my buddy on the Middle East desk," Fred said, his eyes glued to the skimpy triangle of cloth that covered the girl's rear end. "He said Roger Sherman was stirring things up over you. Seems Sherman got upset over a visit you and some broad paid him, and called out the cavalry. They're out to shut you down, Pete."

"Too late," I said. "Did and done."

I told him about the visits to Sidney, Jo and Sanders, and about losing my magazine assignment. When I finished, the cigar hung loosely in his lips, his eyes still on the girl ahead. She turned and glanced at him. He smiled again. She returned the smile but hurried on.

"Damn," Fred said.

I wasn't certain whether the oath was directed at the visitations or the girl.

"Your friends must be pissed at you," I said. "Sorry I got you involved."

Fred took the cigar from his mouth and spat gray smoke.

"Hell, Pete," he said. "That's why I'm here. Like I told you, I feel responsible."

I watched his face, trying to fathom what he meant. It was impossible. Fred's face looked carved from rock. I held my hand out, stopped him and made him face me.

"What are you telling me, Fred?"

"My buddy's just delighted," he said. "The whole agency's just happier than an old bull put to stud."

He motioned me off the boardwalk, and we sat on the short beach wall that looked out over the ocean. Fred took one last lingering look at the girl in the bikini before she disappeared into the crowd.

"Now I don't know everything there is to know about this here Project Qari you've been asking about, but I do know The Company was against it from the start," he said, taking the cigar from his lips. "The pros all thought it carried too much baggage, that there'd be hell to pay if word of it ever leaked out. So the White House went out of channels to get this thing rolling. From what my friend says, it was a royal screw up from the start. Made Iran-Contra look like the Normandy invasion. They don't think too highly of Colonel Roger Sherman."

I suddenly felt like an old whore, used and abused.

"The CIA wanted Qari exposed," I said. "That's it, isn't it? They've been using me."

Fred stuck the cigar back in his mouth, shoved his hands into his pockets and nodded slowly.

"They wanted the shit to hit the fan so they could move in and discredit Sherman and others like him," he said. "You hear this stuff about taking covert ops away from The Company?"

I nodded.

"If Qari's exposed, The Company can show it's the only government agency reliable and responsible enough to run covert ops," he said. "All these new spook agencies, most of them not even on the books—they ain't my kind of people, Pete."

Fred dropped the cigar on the walkway and crushed it with his boot. He looked out at the ocean, his face hard, the muscles in his jaw rigid.

"These guys don't have any rule book to play by, no oversight committee," he said. "It's like the old cowboy days in the Agency. They don't care who they hurt." He shook his head. "I tell you, it scares even me."

"If it scares you, Fred, imagine how I feel."

"You should, too, partner."

A shiver ran through me even though the air was warm. I didn't need Fred to tell me I should be scared. I realized I'd been scared for days. But now I knew why.

"Sherman and his buddies must've put the narcs up to raiding my place," I said. "When that didn't work, they decided to dry up my sources."

Fred look at me, his eyes narrow slits. I told him about the brick planted in my toilet and the street team raid. I glanced down the beach at the public restrooms and wondered if the trash there had been emptied yet.

"Sounds like Sherman," Fred said. "Rumors were he was involved with moving some shit during Iran-Contra."

Fred took a deep breath, and let it out slowly. He glanced at his watch.

"Look, partner," he said. "Things get too hot, you call me, hear? Like I said, I feel responsible. You need me, I'll cover your six. Deal?"

I nodded and thanked him.

"Meantime, Pete, you watch your ass."

§

I walked back to the bungalow, detouring to check my box at the post office. Bills, self-addressed and stamped envelopes bearing rejected story queries, and a large manila envelope with no return address. I paid them little attention as I walked the rest of the way home. My mind reeled with the events of the day and Fred's warning.

There comes a time in preparing every story when a reporter has to decide whether it's really worth pursuing. Sometimes after days of research, you simply determine there's no real story there. You drop it and cut your losses. Sometimes, pursuing a story is just too costly in time and money, a major consideration for self-employed journalists like me who only earn piecemeal pay for the stories they sell. Other times, a story was just too damn dangerous to pursue.

In this case, there was definitely a story to tell, but no way to tell it. It would be useless to pursue it unless I found a new buyer. Perhaps Marsha Hand would come through. Yet I had to admit to myself I was getting pretty spooked. It would be more than simple to just turn my back and walk away from it, it'd be the smart thing to do. No one would think the lesser of me, I told myself.

Or would they?

I heard Jo's voice asking me again if I was going to drop the story, and I knew then there was no way I could drop it. Instead, I hurried home hoping Marsha had called.

The little red light on the message machine blinked at me indicating she had. I tossed the mail on the desk unopened and pushed the playback button.

"Pete, Marsha Hand. Call me."

Her message didn't make me hopeful. I slumped in the desk chair and dialed the L.A. number.

"Sorry, Pete," Marsha told me. "New York is shy about Iraqi stories now. There's just been so much recently. Readers are getting bored."

"Bored?" I heard my voice rising. I was tired, angry, and losing control of my emotions. "Jesus, Marsha. This story's bigger than Watergate "

"Pete, the home editors said if you wanted to file a story advisory they'd look at it," Marsha said. "If they thought it was worth pursuing, though, they'd pass it on to the Washington bureau. You'd get a finder's fee, of course."

"A finder's fee?"

I gripped the phone so tightly I could hear the plastic cracking. I took a deep breath and tried to control my anger. I couldn't afford losing my contract with the news magazine. It provided most of my income.

"Listen, Marsha," I said, trying to loosen my jaw so my words sounded normal. "Thanks for trying. But I think I'll take this elsewhere, if I can."

"Sure, Pete," she said. "But you know how it is."

"Yeah, if it's not happening in New York or DC, it's not happening."

"That about sums it up."

When the line went dead, I stared out the window, the phone still grasped tightly in my hand. I racked my brain for another possible market. But to find one, I would have to go through an elaborate and time-consuming querying process. Then I remembered the one standing offer I had, the one I had been trying not to remember. Reluctantly, I put the phone down, and rummaged through the desk drawer for the card Larrs gave me. He was in, but getting ready to go out with a camera crew to do an interview. I told him I was ready to accept his offer.

"Oh, really," he said, feigning disinterest. "*San Diego Life* screw you over?"

"You offered me more money."

"That was then, Brandt."

I didn't need to play games with Larrs.

"Fine," I said, pulling my own bluff. "Then I'll just take this to the newsweekly I string for."

"Not so fast, Brandt," Larrs said quickly. "I'm just being cautious here. I don't even know what I'm buying. But I made you an offer, and I'll stand by it—if I think the story's worth it."

"It's worth more," I said.

"Good." Larrs' voice changed to the ah-shucks-I'm-just-one-of-the-guys diction he used on air. "Look, I trust you, Brandt. Really I do. You're a damn good reporter and I respect you for that. Just don't try screwing me like you did before."

"This is business, Larrs," I told him. "And it's a story that'll make us famous."

"Us?"

"I want half credit as well as cash."

"Is it that big?"

"Bigger."

The line was silent for a while. I let it stay that way.

"Okay, call me tomorrow," Larrs finally said. "It better be big."

"It is," I said. Then I hung up.

I had a bad taste in my mouth, the same one I always got around Larrs. Not only didn't I like dealing with the man, but I also felt I had lowered myself to his level in demanding credit on the story. Walking to the kitchen, I made myself a Scotch and water. Then I went into the bedroom and lit a cigarette from my nightmare stash. I felt guilty about both.

Back at the desk, I sipped the drink and smoked the cigarette and looked dully at the mail. The bills made me feel a little better about cutting a deal with Larrs, but not much. I picked up the manila envelope, looked it over, then opened it. Inside was a two-inch thick photocopy of the Pentagon report on the friendly fire incident that killed Robert Stanning. Clipped to it was a torn sheet of Marine Corps stationary with no name or unit designation. Typed on the stationary were two words: Semper Fi.

Paul Polmar had come through.

I spent the afternoon reading the report. When I finished, I understood what happened that night in the Iraqi desert. I knew why Polmar was ordered to fire on the MP vehicles, and I knew who gave the order. I knew why Stanning died. And what's more, I knew the name of the lone survivor of the attack.

After staring at the wall for some time, I went back into the kitchen and made another drink, stronger this time. Then I lit another cigarette.

This time I didn't feel guilty at all.

CHAPTER 23

W hat's wrong?"
We were eating Chinese take-out again. She was looking at me over the rim of her wine glass, her blue eyes cool and appraising. I shook my head and went on chewing my Kung Pao chicken.

"Peter," Jo said. "Something's bothering you. You've barely spoken all night. Is it losing the magazine assignment? The creeps harassing people?" She lowered the glass and tilted her head. "Is it last night?"

I shook my head again. "No."

"Peter, talk to me, damn it."

I was going to wait until after dinner to tell her. Somehow, I guess I hoped she would tell me first. However, I could see it wasn't going to work that way. I put down the chopsticks, drained my wine glass, then stood and got the report. I laid it on the table between us and sat down, keeping my hand on it.

"Paul Polmar came through," I told her. "This is the secret Pentagon report on the fratricide incident Robert Stanning was killed in."

"What?"

Jo's eyes grew wide. She reached for the photocopy, but I keep my hand on it. She leaned back and looked at me curiously. I picked it up and flipped through the pages.

"I don't know how Polmar got this," I said. "It was meant only for top brass consumption. I suspect someone sent it to him the way he sent it to me."

"Peter, can I read it, please?"

Jo's hand reached out. Her face held a look of puzzlement.

"Peter?"

"Sure you can," I said. "I guess you've got the right since you're mentioned in it."

Jo's face went slack. Her eyes dulled. She leaned back in the chair, her eyes staring at the plate on the table.

"So you know?" she said.

"How you were really wounded?" She nodded. "I know."

"Peter "

"Polmar told the radio station three army MPs were killed in the attack," I said. "He didn't know about Robert Stanning until someone sent him this report. Nor did he know there were four MPs in the vehicles he attacked—three enlisted and one officer. The officer was severely wounded, but survived."

"Pe—"

I slammed the report down on the table hard enough to make the plates and glasses jump. Jo jumped, too.

"Why the hell didn't you tell me you were wounded in that attack? What the hell has this charade been all about?"

"Peter, please "

"I should have known," I said. "Last night, when you said people you were responsible for died. And the other night when the nightmare woke you up, you were having a flashback to the attack."

I kicked back the chair and paced the floor.

"What is it with you, Jo?" I demanded. "You have a problem with telling the truth, lady? First, you're JoAnne the stripper. Next, you're Cold As Ice Rice, security officer. Now this. Just who the hell are you really, Jo? Or have you been dealing with army lies for so long you don't remember?"

As Jo stared at me, the ice came back into her eyes. She slowly took the napkin from her lap and laid it on the table.

"Fine," she said, standing. "I think I should leave."

She walked to the door and turned.

"You weren't there, Peter," she said, her face hard as the armor on a tank. "It wasn't your men killed in the attack. You weren't responsible for them. You didn't have to watch their deaths brushed under the carpet in some bureaucratic shell game. What I've done, Peter, I've done for them—Mitchell, Alvarez, and Vaccaro. I'm sorry I lied to you, Peter. But after everything that's happened, I don't know whom to trust. I don't know who my friends are."

Jo opened the door, still looking at me. I said nothing.

"Fine," Jo said quietly. She turned and opened the door wider.

"Jo."

She stopped and turned around. I was to her in two steps, pushing the door shut.

"I'm your friend," I told her. "I'm on your side."

The ice in her eyes melted a bit. I cupped her chin and kissed her, then we held each until our heart beats slowed to normal. Jo cried softly on my shoulder.

"Jo," I said, "tell me what really happened, okay?"

Jo pulled backed and ran a knuckle beneath one eye. Then she looked at me and nodded.

§

So she told me, her eyes wide and dark and focused on some distant battleground. She was reliving the horrors of that night, and it was all the more terrifying for her because she knew the outcome, like watching a train you knew was heading for a collapsed bridge and knowing you were unable to stop it. I tried to put my arm around her to comfort her, but she squirmed away. She was back there again, with her men in the war zone and there was no room for being weak or soft. No room for being a woman. So I sat in the chair next to the couch and listened.

"Some advanced units found Stanning in an Iraqi field hospital," she said. "When our own field medics arrived, they judged his condition too critical for their care. Our advance was so fast, the logistics couldn't keep up and the medevac choppers were out of range. So my major ordered me to take two vehicles and transport Stanning closer to our own lines where the choppers could get to us. To be truthful, I think he was nervous having a woman that far into Iraqi territory. Ironic, considering what happened, huh?"

I nodded and she continued.

"Mitchell was my Humvee driver and I asked Alvarez and Vaccaro to follow in their Bradley with Stanning. Vaccaro had advanced first aid training, so I figured they were the best crew for the job. Besides . . ." Jo smiled slightly. "I liked them. Mitch, too. I felt comfortable with them. They always harangued me about being a woman, but it was just fun. When it came down to the job, they didn't seem to mind. We worked well together."

Jo's eyes drifted to the floor. "I miss them," she said softly.

She took a deep breath and let it out in a slow sigh. Then she focused again on that night in the desert.

"It was so dark, Peter," she said. "No moon and the stars were hidden by the smoke from the oil fires. You could just see the glow of the fires beyond the horizon beneath the pall of smoke, but you still couldn't see anything where we were. It was eerie. We drove by compass bearing and the glow on the horizon alone.

"I was scared. I know Mitch was, too. He always talked when he got frightened. Jesus, that man could talk. But he was a good man. Just scared. Like me. We all were. I could hear it in Alvarez's voice on the radio, too. But we just kept going like we were supposed to."

Jo looked at me, her eyes questioning. "I've heard that's the definition of courage. To keep on going even though you're scared to death."

I nodded.

"Then they were brave men," she said. "Boys, really. Mitch was the oldest at 22. Alvarez was only 19."

She fell silent, lost within her own feelings of loss and regret. I let her mourn before prodding her on.

"Jo," I said quietly. "Tell me what happened."

Her hands covered her face. She looked embarrassed, except for the eyes. Her eyes had grown hollow, like the eyes of soldiers who had seen too much fighting. It was a look I'd seen even in my own eyes.

"I had dysentery and started to get another attack. I stopped the vehicles and went off into the dark to dig myself a hole. You know what I mean?" She waited for me to nod. "Anyway, I was heading back to the Humvee when the attack came."

Her eyes now focused on something I couldn't see, something in the dark of that night that filled her with horror.

"I didn't even hear the choppers," she said. "All I could hear was the sound of the vehicles idling in the dark. Then I saw the streak of the first missile . . ."

I tried to imagine what she was seeing in the eye of her memory. The flaming trail of the deadly dart lighting the pitch-black night, the impact and the fiery explosion. But all I could see was the terror in her eyes.

"I didn't even have time to scream," Jo continued. "I heard Mitch yell 'incoming'—he must've have been standing next to the Humvee. Then it hit. It was almost like slow motion. That was all I saw before I was thrown backward. I think that's when I was hit."

Jo unconsciously rubbed her injured leg.

"Shrapnel and burning fuel. I heard the second missile hit the Bradley as I was falling over and rolling. Then I heard the screams."

She was trying to swallow hard and not succeeding. She looked around for something to help her. I took her glass from the table, filled it with more wine, and handed it to her. She drank it all in one gulp. I filled it again and this time she drank half of it before continuing.

"The screams, Peter," she said. "The screams. They weren't human. Not like anything I ever heard. Then the choppers flew over. Their rotors sent sand slashing into my face, my wound. They seemed to whip up the flames devouring the vehicles. I screamed at them. I knew they had to be ours. The Eye-racks couldn't put a kite in the sky without it being shot down. I screamed until they went away, until the only sound left was my own screaming. Then I looked at the vehicles and saw the bodies."

Jo grabbed the wine glass again, drained it, and held it out for refilling. I took the bottle and my own glass from the dining table, filled hers, then mine. Tears welled up in Jo's eyes and overflowed. Dark rivulets ran across her tanned cheeks. She didn't try to wipe them away.

"Mitch was on the ground in front of the Humvee," she continued. "His body was burning, what was left of it. Part of one arm was gone and his head—the back of his head was gone, too. I could see it in the fire light.

"The Bradley was burning, too, and there was a body hanging out of the driver's hatch. It must have been Alvarez. Those Bradleys are made of aluminum. Did you know aluminum burns? It burns hot, too. Alvarez was hanging there and there was already nothing left but scorched bones and tissue. One bony arm was still stretched out as if he was reaching for me and—oh, God, Peter, his chest had exploded! His ribs were spread out like gruesome fingers. Someone told me later that's what happens when you breathe in super-heated gases. My God, do you know what that means? He was still alive when it happened!"

That was it. She couldn't hold it back anymore. I moved in and put my arms around Jo and this time she didn't move away. She pressed her head deep into my neck and let go with all the anguish and pain she had bottled up. I held her and stroked her hair. Her body heaved against mine. I wanted to say something that would comfort her, heal her, but I knew too well no words would ever do that. So I did all I could do, and just held her.

How ironic, I thought as I held her, that Jo and I traveled similar journeys by vastly dissimilar courses. Like her, I wanted to prove myself in war. Even after the death of my brother in Vietnam, I knew I needed to see battle myself. When the chance came to cover the fighting in El Salvador and Nicaragua, I jumped at it like a panther on its prey. I soon learned there was little more to war than fear and horror, and the things I saw etched my soul with scars that would never truly heal. Now Jo suffered the cost of pursuing vainglory.

Later, after the tears had gone and she had washed her face in the bathroom, she sat back down and told me the rest of the story.

"I woke up in a field hospital," she said. "My leg felt like it was on fire. After a couple of days, my CO came to see me. He told me Mitchell, Alvarez, and Vaccaro were already shipped home for burial. He said each of us was getting the Purple Heart and the Bronze Star. I looked at him like he was crazy but he just sort of looked away and cleared his throat.

"I said, 'Sir, we were hit by friendly fire.' And he said, 'That's not how it's going down, Rice. Mitch and the others, their families were told they were killed in action. And you're WIA.' I told him I saw the choppers, I could see their silhouettes in the fire light. They were Marine Cobras. And he just said, 'Rice, you were hurt bad, in shock. You really aren't sure what you saw, are you?'"

Jo cupped the wine glass in both hands and held it to her lips. Her hair was damp around the edges from washing her face. It stuck to her forehead and the edges of her ears. Without makeup, she looked like a young girl, except for her eyes, which had grown red from crying and hard from experience.

"Then I asked about the civilian on board and he just looked at me. I asked again and he said, 'There was no civilian on board either vehicle, Rice.' Then he added, 'You remember that and you'll be okay.' He had this strange look of regret on his face, then he patted my good leg and walked away with his head bowed like an old man. I never saw him again. I heard he put in for retirement when he got back to the States."

Her head moved slowly from side to side, her eyes on the floor. She took a deep breath and let it out slowly, then took a sip of wine.

"For a while, I thought the army was just trying to cover up the attack because there had been so many friendly fire incidents during the war. But that didn't explain why they were denying Stanning was with us.

"Then I got a visit from an old friend from officer candidate school. She'd gone into army intelligence and she'd come across some information about the attack. She had been studying some captured Iraqi intel reports on intercepts of our radio traffic when she came across a reference to the attack. It indicated Polmar's flight was ordered to attack my vehicles by someone in CCOMS. It outraged her so much she wanted me to know about it.

"I started making some queries about CCOMS and ConEl. I started thinking maybe the Pentagon didn't want their super new weapons system implicated in a fratricide. Then one day I decided to go straight to the source and called ConEl long distance. The receptionist somehow got confused when I asked to talk to someone about the company's role in Desert Storm. She suddenly sounded nervous and started telling me that Robert Stanning no longer worked for ConEl and hadn't worked there for more than a year. But I hadn't asked for Stanning. Until she told me, I didn't even know he'd ever worked for ConEl."

Jo sipped the wine and brushed the damp hair off her forehead. She seemed to scan the ceiling for some insight and, finding none, continued with her story.

"I decided I was going to find out what happened that night and why. And I didn't give a damn about army cover-ups or whatever. I was placed on limited duty because of my wound and was being reassigned from my MP company. While I was waiting for new orders, I started asking more questions about ConEl and Stanning. One day a detailer I knew told me there was a security liaison post open at ConEl and asked if I was interested. Of course, I said I was."

Jo looked at me, smiled, and shrugged. "You know what happened with Sweeney. Then I met you at the Launch Pad."

I watched her without speaking until she got nervous and shrugged again. She emptied her glass and set it on the coffee table.

"So is there anything in that report that can shed light on what happened?"

I picked up the photocopy and laid it on my lap.

"Polmar already told me he was vectored to your position by radio controllers and ordered to attack," I said. I patted the report. "This confirms it was ordered by CCOMS."

Jo blinked and stared at me with disbelief, her head shaking. "That's all it says? It doesn't say who or why?"

I shook my head. "Not in so many words."

I wasn't certain I should tell her what I knew, or what I thought I knew. As I watched her face, however, I saw disappointment rush into it and sensed the defeat she was feeling, and I felt in myself a flush of emotion I hadn't felt in years. I breathed deeply and sighed.

"But I think I can tell you," I said.

CHAPTER 24

Funny how bad things happen on beautiful days. The Japanese attacked Pearl Harbor on a bright Sunday morning as GIs and sailors lounged in their bunks trying to decide what to do with their day off. It was warm and clear that day JFK rode through the streets of Dallas with the top down on his Lincoln convertible, and wearing sunglasses as if he were riding to the beach instead of to his fate. It was that kind of a morning when Jo and I drove to ConEl to confront Roger Sherman. The sun rose like a fiery comet over the eastern hills and took the sky all to itself. Despite the warmth and beauty of the day, as I climbed from Jo's truck I had an unshakable feeling something terrible was about to happen.

It did.

I had explained my suspicions to Jo the night before. She listened first with disbelief, then growing anger. When we went to bed, she made love with urgent desperation as if that would be our last night together. Vicious images of burning corpses filled my sleep, some inspired by Jo's description of what happened that night in the desert, others inspired by what I had seen on my own battlegrounds. I woke frequently, and in the hours before dawn, I found myself alone in bed. I could see Jo across the room, silhouetted against the window, staring outside in silence.

After breakfast, we stopped at Jo's apartment so she could change into her uniform. We barely spoke as we drove to Kearny Mesa and the ConEl facility. I concentrated on what I was going to say to Sherman. Jo seemed distracted by thoughts too distant for me to understand. When we parked, she looked at me and squeezed my hand, smiling.

"Let's go get the bastard," she said.

She stepped out of the truck and slammed the door, stuck a large, unwieldy black purse under her arm, and marched toward the admin building with me in lock step. Inside the sealed building, the conditioned air was cool but stuffy with the breath and odors of hundreds of workers locked inside. Jo led the way to Sherman's office on the third floor, but I knew when we had found it long before we reached it. Standing outside, backs to the door and hands clasped, were two large men in blue, lightweight windbreakers. Each had an earphone coiling from his collar.

"Godzilla and King Kong, I presume," I murmured to Jo. Both men seemed to recognize us. Their mouths formed sardonic grins. They shifted position as we approached the office and blocked the door.

"Colonel Sherman is busy," one of them said. He wore dark slacks and had the satisfied countenance of a bully. I decided he must be Godzilla. The other wore jeans and had a simian look to him. I called him King Kong.

"So are we," I said. "So either open the door and announce us like good little doormen, or get new jobs."

Godzilla and King Kong both sighed impatiently. I wondered if they learned to do that together, like learning to march in step. Neither moved from the door.

Sherman's office had a large picture window that looked out into the corridor. Closed blinds sealed off the window. I looked at Jo, then glanced around the hallway. Through the open door of one of the offices, I saw something that gave me an idea. I marched in, nodded to a man in shirtsleeves as he looked up from behind his desk, took his coat from a standing rack, and laid it gently across the back of a guest chair. Then I picked up the coat rack.

"I'll bring it right back," I assured him.

Carrying the coat rack like a battering ram, I walked back to Sherman's office and positioned myself in front of the window.

"We either go through the door or the window," I said, knowing I was mad enough to do it. "Choice is yours."

Godzilla rolled his eyes while King Kong watched me with bemusement. I shifted my grip on the rack and tested the window with a tap. Then another tap, harder. The third tap nearly shattered the pane. The bemusement went out of both men's faces.

"What the hell is going on out here?"

Sherman opened the door. The overhead fluorescent light glinted off his baldpate. He was in shirtsleeves, his tie loosened and collar open. He looked at Godzilla and King Kong, saw Jo, then saw me.

"Oh," he said, as if he understood everything he saw. "Now what the hell do you two want?"

"An invitation would do," I said.

"We want to talk to you, Sherman," Jo said.

"I'm busy." His mouth twisted snidely at one corner. "Make an appointment with my secretary. She's right down the hallway." He turned to me. "And I don't have anything to say to this reporter."

He managed to make it sound like I belonged to some caste beneath his own station.

"I think you do, Sherman."

I tossed the coat rack to King Kong. He caught it expertly at port arms and stiffened, as if standing for inspection.

"Like about your role in the murder of Robert Stanning and three army MPs."

A fourth man appeared at the door. He was shorter than Sherman, and wore a suit and rimless glasses. He looked at me, then Jo. I saw the glint of recognition in both their eyes.

"I told you, Brandt, I never knew Stanning," Sherman said. "Besides, I understand he was accidently killed by friendly fire."

Godzilla stepped forward, placing himself between Sherman and me. He looked at me in a way to make me felt small, which he did with the same expertise that his friend did the manual of arms with a coat rack.

"You heard the colonel," he said. He put his hand none too lightly on my shoulder. "It'd be better if y'all left right now."

"Don't touch me," I growled.

A tolerant smile crossed Godzilla's lips. He looked as if nothing would make him happier than for me to try something with him. I smiled back just as tolerantly.

"If I'm crazy enough to go through his window," I said, "imagine what I'm crazy enough to do to you."

The smile slipped from Godzilla's face, but only for a moment. He stepped closer to me, his chest nearly butting into mine. My eyes came to his mouth. His breath was bad.

"You just blew it anyway, Sherman," I said. "The official story is Stanning was killed by Allied bombing. Only a handful of people knew he died when Marine choppers attacked Captain Rice's MP convoy. If you really didn't know Stanning, how would you know that?"

It was just enough to bluff them. Sherman and the man in the suit glared at each other. Godzilla and King Kong looked at each other as if they hadn't realized they were protecting a possible murderer, let alone someone who had possibly murdered fellow service members. King Kong looked at the coat rack and set it down gently, then looked at Sherman. The colonel smiled calmly.

"There you go talking nonsense again, Brandt," he said. "If Stanning and these others were killed by helicopters, how the hell was I involved in it?"

"The choppers were merely the gun, Sherman." I stepped away from Godzilla and moved next to Jo. "You pulled the trigger."

Sherman looked at the man in the suit, then they both looked at the two phony feds. Godzilla and King Kong glared at all of us.

"Who's the suit?" I asked Jo.

"My friend allegedly from CID," she whispered.

The phony CID man looked at us, then back to the two thugs. He buttoned the middle button of his coat and turned to Sherman.

"I'll take care of this, major," Sherman said, nodding toward Jo and me. He gestured to Godzilla and King Kong. "You talk to them."

The major stepped from the door and gestured to the two thugs. Godzilla and King Kong coldly glared at me as they passed, but the fact they gave Sherman the same look warmed me up again. Sherman studied Jo and me a moment longer, then pushed the door open wider.

"Well," he said. "I guess I have no choice, do I?"

Sherman's office was the size of a small hotel suite. The desk was large and made of highly varnished oak, topped with a gold and leather pen set, a leather-edged blotter and one of those computerized telephones no one can ever figure out how to work. There were no papers on the desk, no sign of a harried business executive. The walls were beige with a dark trim and hung with photographs of fighter jets and bombers. There was a file cabinet against one wall with a locked bolt running through the drawer handles. A little cardboard sign hanging from the lock read: LOCKED. The outer wall was all windows, but the blinds were pulled, leaving the office looking dark despite the fluorescent lighting.

We followed Sherman inside and stood at his desk while he went behind it. He started to sit, looked at us standing there and gestured gallantly for us to seat ourselves.

"Now what's this little fantasy of yours, Brandt?"

Sherman hooked one leg over the top of his desk, trying to look nonchalant.

"No fantasy, Sherman," I said. "No more than Project Qari."

Sherman frowned and moved his shoulders around in a shrug.

"Too late to play ignorant, colonel," I told him. "You had your chance in the gym and you blew it."

"Brandt, I still have no fucking idea what in hell you're talking about," Sherman said, swinging his leg off the desk. He leaned his hands on the desk and glared at me. "Let me see if I can say this slowly enough for you to understand. I never met this guy Stanning and I didn't kill him. I have no idea what this Project What's-It is, and I still don't have to listen to this garbage from you."

He turned to Jo and leaned farther across the desk.

"And you, captain, had better learn when to cut your losses and run," he hissed. "Continuing to deal with this—" Sherman glanced at me, his mouth turned down with distaste. "—this nut case can only look bad on your record."

Jo's eyes were already frigid orbs of blue. It was hard to imagine they could be any colder, but as she stared back at Sherman an iciness came to them that sent shivers down even my own spine.

"Damn my record, you bastard," Jo said, her voice as cold as her stare. "You murdered my men."

Sherman leaned back in his chair. The lines at his mouth grew deeper as he studied Jo.

"I wouldn't be so eager to hurl accusations, captain," he said. "Official records are precarious in nature. They can easily change overnight." Sherman picked up a silver ballpoint pen and tapped his desk. "For instance, I seem to recall you were not even with your men when they were attacked. Correct? Malingering in wartime is a serious offense. Desertion even more so."

"Worse than desertion, colonel," I jumped in, "is treason."

The pen in Sherman's hand stopped tapping. It hung suspended at an angle above the desktop while Sherman's charcoal eyes shot flames at me. Sherman's grasp began to bend the pen as his mouth dipped into a deeper frown.

"What would you know about patriotism or treason, Brandt?" he growled.

I stared back at Sherman, my face a rocky mask. My breathing slowed, as if I were entering a trance. I had hit a sensitive spot in Sherman's armor, and now I was going to exploit it.

"Aiding and abetting the enemy in wartime is treason by anybody's definition, Sherman," I said. "And that's exactly what Project Qari came to be, wasn't it? And you were the man who orchestrated it."

A small tick appeared at the corner of Sherman's mouth. It sent fleshy tremors up the crevices bordering his lips. His tongue began to work the inside of his mouth. But he said nothing, and his glare lost none of its fire.

"Washington was officially neutral during the Iran-Iraq War," I continued. "But Washington was actually scared to death of an Iranian victory. The Reagan administration decided to help Iraq. First a little intelligence. Then a couple of photos from spy satellites. Then finally, materiel like weapons technology, and even *hard rice*—weapons. That's where you came in Sherman, straight from your disgrace in Iran-Contra.

"Washington needed someone with a special operations background to run Qari, someone who was expendable and deniable. Most people figured your career was over after Iran-Contra. You were publicly passed over for promotion to general, and assigned to ConEl as project officer for CCOMS. Normally that's a one-way ticket, a waiting room for retirees-to-be. And that's exactly what it was supposed to look like.

"In fact, you used your position at ConEl to orchestrate Project Qari, including ConEl's role in it. If Qari was ever exposed, it'd be written off as the work of an embittered officer, another loose cannon like Ollie North. Plausible deniability, they call it."

Sherman still didn't move. He looked like a statue, with the exception of his burning charcoal eyes and the slight sheen of sweat forming on his baldhead. When he spoke, his lips barely moved.

"You're going too far now, Brandt."

"Not me," I replied, shaking my head. "But you did, didn't you?"

There was no response, so I went on.

"Robert Stanning was your mule, your foot man. He set up all the false front companies you used to smuggle hardware into Iraq. When Washington pulled the plug on Qari at the start of the Gulf crisis, you sent Stanning to Europe to close down operations there. But Washington started thinking a weakened Iraq wasn't in its best interests. Iran's Islamic fundamentalism still scared them, you see. So the stop order on Qari was pulled. That's when you ordered Stanning to Iraq, to reinitiate contacts there. Unfortunately, Stanning got wounded in an Allied bombing raid on Basra. When he was discovered wounded, you had him killed." I watch a rivulet of sweat roll down from the top of Sherman's head into his closely cropped hair.

"It took me a while to figure out why you would kill your own man, but not too long. I only had to reach back into my own experience covering the Contras in Nicaragua. It was the Hasenfus debacle all over again, wasn't it?"

I wasn't sure, but I thought a saw of glint of admiration flash through Sherman's eyes. It was the look of a madman when he finds someone who understands his ramblings.

"That was it," I said.

Jo turned to me, the question clear in her eyes.

"Gene Hasenfus was the sole survivor of a cargo plane shot down over Nicaragua while dropping supplies to the Contra rebels," I told her. "It was all part of Ronald Reagan's Iran-Contra dealings. Hasenfus and the other members of his crew were part of the secret supply operation the White House put together—outside of channels, as they like to say. When he was captured, it blew the cover off of Iran-Contra."

Sherman had a distant look on his face. Wherever he was, he wasn't happy being there again. I didn't blame him.

"Colonel Sherman here was the man who orchestrated the drops," I said. "He hired Hasenfus and the others. When everything went to hell, his career went with it. Does that sum it up pretty concisely, colonel?"

Sherman was back in the present. He smiled bitterly.

"Quite concisely, Brandt," he said.

"When the Pentagon decided to put CCOMS into operation during the Gulf War, you had to accompany it along with the ConEl technicians," I continued. "On the night Jo's convoy was attacked, you were operations officer aboard CCOMS. Isn't that right, colonel?"

He flicked his hand as if brushing away a fly and leaned back in his chair.

"I'm not at liberty to discuss my duties during Desert Storm," he said. "I was in special operations, Brandt. Even you can understand that."

"But you weren't assigned to special ops anymore," I countered. "I've seen a copy of the secret Pentagon report on the attack, Sherman."

I fudged a little, not wanting him to know I had a copy of the report. If I were treading on sensitive ground, Sherman didn't seem to know it. He remained annoyingly passive. But the slick crown of his head seemed to glisten ever so slightly more.

"You're listed as a member of the crew that night."

"Does this all have a point, Brandt?" Sherman asked. He casually looked at his watch. "I have a racquetball appointment in half an hour."

"Let it wait," I said.

That got a rise from him. A man long used to giving and taking orders, Sherman obviously considered disrespect out of line, particularly coming from a lower life form like a reporter. His charcoal-fired eyes heated with intensity again, and the muscles at the back of his jaw tensed and formed a rigid bulge.

"Where was I?" I said. "Right. The Pentagon report. CCOMS' computer system maintains a highly detailed record of everything that transpires on tape. Did you know that, colonel?"

"Of course I did," Sherman said, adding a sigh of impatience. "The system is designed to provide a computer re-enactment of all missions for after-action debriefing and simulation training."

"Spoken like a true Pentagon bureaucrat," I said, grinning. Sherman didn't return the grin. I glanced at Jo. She wasn't smiling either. I cleared my throat and went on.

"The mission tapes from that night show Jo's little convoy was properly identified as a friendly on the computer screens used by the controllers. Then something strange happened. Just before the order to attack was sent to Captain Polmar, the symbols on the screens changed. Jo's convoy was designated as a hostile."

Sherman's shoulders moved an inch up and down. "It got confusing up there some times," he said. "We were tracking and trying to identify hundreds—no, thousands of radar contacts over hundreds of square miles. Even with CCOMS' vast array of electronics it was still confusing."

"I'll bet," I said. "But most of those targets were in another operational sector. The area Jo and her men were in was fairly empty of contacts. Or so the investigation report says. Captain Polmar said the same thing. That's why he didn't want to fire."

"The report also says there was a glitch in the software," Sherman said. "It was a new and untried system. There are always glitches." The colonel leaned forward and looked at Jo, his hands held open before him. "You want me to apologize, captain? Then I apologize. *Mea culpa.*"

Sherman sat back with a grunt and crossed his arms. Jo gave him a look that could have sent Satan in searching of woolly underwear.

"That's what the investigators concluded," I continued, "but the facts stated in the report don't support it. The mission tapes record that just 15 minutes before the order to fire was given, someone at an unmanned console changed the convoy's designation from friendly to hostile. It wasn't a glitch and it wasn't human error, because no one was manning that console. It was intentional."

"Get to your fucking point, Brandt," Sherman growled.

Something about his eyes told me he knew damn well what my point was going to be. The burning coals had died out, leaving them looking dead and desiccated.

"There was a small fire aboard CCOMS just before the attack," I said. "One of those bags used for destroying classified material. What do you call them?"

"A burn bag," Jo said.

"Yeah, a burn bag somehow caught fire. While everyone was distracted by that, the convoy's designation got changed."

"I'm still waiting for your point, Brandt," Sherman said.

"The point is this," I said. "You heard the radio communications between CCOMS and Jo's MP unit. You heard the name Robert Stanning and you knew what had happened. And then you remembered the Hasenfus debacle. You weren't going to let that happen again. So you started the fire to create a distraction and when no one was looking, you changed the designation on Jo's convoy. When the fire was out, you gave the order to Polmar's helicopter patrol to close in and destroy the convoy."

"That's incredible!" Sherman said, with a laugh that sounded more like a bark. "Absolutely incredible. Don't you think someone maybe noticed the icon changed and would have said something?"

Sherman smiled, the grooves on his face deepening into half circles. But his forehead glistened even more with perspiration.

"According to the report, someone did. When Polmar hesitated to fire, one of controllers supported him. The controller told you he was certain the blips on the screen had been friendly forces. But you issued the order to fire again."

Tires squealed in the parking lot outside. Sherman and I instinctively turned toward the shaded window. When Sherman turned back around, his eyes widened momentarily, then his lips formed a cruel smile.

"You're not going to use that, captain," he said.

Jo stood before the desk, legs braced apart, arms extended. In her hands was an army-issued 9mm Beretta automatic. Her purse lay opened on the floor. Her face was a rigid mask of hatred and the look in her eyes scared me.

"Jo…"

"Forget it, Peter," she said. "This bastard's not going to get away with it."

Sherman's vicious smile deepened. "Yes, I will," he said.

The colonel stood and opened the window blinds. The sun glared through like an arc lamp. It bathed Jo's face, showing taut ridges where her veins and arteries were pumping blood with frenetic force, and where the muscles in her jaw were tight with tension. When Sherman turned around, he was still smiling. I almost started hoping Jo would blow the smirk right off his face.

"I already have, captain," Sherman continued. He crossed his arms and looked at me. "Your guesswork was pretty much on the mark, Brandt. I'll have to reappraise my opinion of the accuracy of the press."

"So Stanning was your man?"

"In more ways than one," he said. "Oh, don't mourn for Bob Stanning. He wasn't just working for ConEl. He was a professional player. He originally worked for West German intelligence, using his position at ConEl for industrial espionage. That was not nice. Friends aren't supposed to spy on friends. But instead of a messy and embarrassing trial, we simply usurped him—with the blessings of the Bonn government, of course. Sort of lend-lease."

Sherman sat on the edge of his desk and directed his attention to me, ignoring the gun Jo had pointed at his head. Jo glared at him, the gun wavering with each of her breaths. The sun shone through Sherman's white shirt, and despite his relaxed countenance, I could see he was sweating heavily.

"Your guess about the Hasenfus debacle was particularly insightful," he said. "Even those clowns at the Pentagon couldn't understand that. There was a reason we didn't give Hasenfus and the others parachutes. If they were shot down, they were just dead mercenaries, totally deniable. But Hasenfus went against orders and brought his own chute. He lived to answer questions, and the brought the whole Contra operation down." Sherman shook his head. "I was not going to let that happen again with Stanning."

"Dead he was just another unsolved mystery," I said.

"Exactly."

"What about the others?" demanded Jo. The gun in her hand shook badly. "What about Mitchell, Alvarez, and Vacarro?"

"Collateral damage," Sherman said, with a simple shrug. "The price of victory, captain."

Jo's breathing suddenly steadied and so did the gun. Her eyes had turned almost white with cold hatred and contempt. The finger on the trigger tightened. Sherman smiled and shook his head.

me. Whatever it was, the smile disappeared and Sherman began to play dumb.

"What do you mean by that?"

"You killed Jack Sweeney," I said. "You knew Jo was asking questions about Stanning. You knew Sweeney had a guilty conscience after his son was killed by an Iraqi missile—maybe a missile built with technology he helped ConEl supply Baghdad. Maybe you knew Sweeney had agreed to talk to Jo, or maybe you were just afraid he might talk. It was all the same. The Hasenfus fear. So you followed him up to the roof and pushed him off."

"You know, I think I need to reappraise my opinion of reporters again," Sherman said. "You disappoint me."

I shrugged and went on. "Then when you heard I was sniffing around about the Widow Stanning's lawsuit, you decided to get me out of the way. You broke into my place, planted drugs in my toilet and called Lt. Holden on the narcotics street team.

"You owed Holden a favor after he sandbagged an investigation into a smuggling operation being run out of one of the rural airports. The smugglers turned out to be some of your contract pilots. They flew supplies to the Contras and you let them bring whatever they wanted back into the country. So he believed you when you told him there were drugs in my apartment. Bet you wonder what happened to that brick of Thai, don't you? It's probably making some homeless guy at the beach real mellow now."

Sherman's eyes burned angrily again, but there was more perspiration beading on his head. Popping noises came from the outer offices again, louder now. Sherman pushed passed me and headed toward the door.

"Go to hell, Brandt," he said.

"The cops know Sweeney was pushed, colonel," I said. Sherman stopped with his back to me and turned slowly. "The circumstantial evidence is enough to bring you to court and expose the whole game. Face it, it's over."

"I don't think so, Mr. Brandt," Sherman hissed. "The game goes on and it's a very dangerous game. Not one for amateurs to play. Take my warning very seriously."

Another round of popping noises made Sherman curse and turn back to the door. "What the hell is that?" he muttered as he opened the door and walked out.

There was one loud crack, and Sherman stumbled back through the door. In the same instant, the back of his head exploded in a shower of shattered bone, blood, and gray matter. His body fell against me and we both went over. Jo screamed.

I shoved Sherman off me and rose to a crouch. A man in blue jeans and a sweat- and blood-stained T-shirt blocked the door, a high-powered AK-47 assault rifle gripped in both hands.

"Well, hey, Brandt," Sidney Clipper said. "How ya doing?"

CHAPTER 25

Sidney's skin was pale and drawn taut across his face, his lips pulled back in a hideous grimace. His eyes were like deep, empty caves, the blue irises eclipsed by the black of dilated pupils. Red embers burned deep in the back of the caves. I wondered if they were reflections of the light streaming from the window or brimstone's hellish glow. I wasn't sure.

I looked down the barrel of the AK and thought I could see the bullet sliding through it, making a beeline for my head. Then the barrel moved away, the telescopic sight affixed to the rifle flashing brightly as it caught the sunlight.

"Hey, Brandt," Sidney said. "Didn't I tell you someone was gonna do a job on these fuckers?"

The AK held a 30-round banana magazine. Sidney had two more tucked into his waistband. I suddenly understood what had been nagging at me for the past few days. Sid's intense displaced anger, his alcoholism, the small cache of weapons in his closet, even the dartboard with Thomas Hess's photograph. Sidney urged me to attend Hess's visit to ConEl. Why? To witness his work.

Sidney was the sniper who fired the shots at Hess. It came to me like a blind man suddenly seeing light for the first time. Only a blind man would have seen it sooner.

Sidney swung the rifle from me to Jo. She gasped and scuttled back against the desk, her face as tight as Sid's. I could see the muscles in Sidney's hand tense as the trigger finger tightened.

"Sid, no! She's one of us!"

"Heh? What's that mean, Brandt? One of us?"

I wasn't really sure what I meant. I was just talking, not certain if anything I said would work.

"She's helping me with my story, like you are," I said. "We're going to blow the lid off this joint."

Sidney stared at Jo, eager to pull the trigger. But something in my words appealed to him. He smirked and raised the rifle.

"Okay," he said. "I got work to do." He turned as if heading back to his office and headed down the hall. He started whistling something familiar, but distorted and off key. Then he sang the words.

"*Hi ho, hi ho. It's off to work we go.*"

The shooting started again. A woman screamed. A man yelled. The shooting continued.

"My God," Jo said, her voice low and distant. "Oh, my God."

I grabbed Jo's arm and pulled her to her feet. She looked around as if searching for something, but I was in too much of a hurry to get out of there. I pulled her to the door and glanced down the hall. To the right, King Kong and Godzilla lay on the floor, dark red blossoms spreading across their chests. A few feet away, the phony CID man leaned against the wall, his right hand grasping his shattered left shoulder. A trail of blood and tissue ran down the wall to where he sat.

Across the hall, the man with the coat rack sat moaning in his chair. A woman lay crumpled in front of his desk, her face shattered, obviously dead. Farther down the hall, workers stared out their office doors, their faces slack, expectant, like young school children not sure what to do during a fire alarm. Sidney was nowhere in sight. A shot rang down an intersecting corridor and told me where he had gone, and I knew it would just be a matter of minutes before he doubled back and began shooting at the crowd of looky-loos.

"That way," I said, pointing toward Sherman's men. Jo was still dumbly gawking at Sherman's office, not saying a word. I pulled her through the door and pushed her in the direction of King Kong and Godzilla. "You can get your purse later," I said, pushing her again "That way. Try to get help. I've got to go the other way."

"But Pe—"

Another shot cut her off. A man in dress slacks and shirt ran from the hallway where Sidney was shooting. The bullet caught him from behind in the right shoulder, picked him up and whipped him around in the air. He landed with a crack as his jaw hit the tile, blood spurting from his shoulder. Another shot screamed past him and smashed a hole in the wall.

"Go!" I screamed to Jo, and ran off toward the wounded man.

As I hit the intersection of the corridors, I glanced to the right. Two bodies, both men, lay just outside office doors. Sid stood over them, his back to me, the rifle waving side to side as if seeking another target. I grabbed the injured man by the belt and shirt collar and hauled him to his feet.

"Run!" I screamed.

I didn't need to tell him twice. Another bullet whined angrily by and we both clocked record times running down the hallway, me still grasping his collar and belt.

"Get back!" I yelled at the looky-loos. "Get back inside and barricade your doors."

They stared at me wide-eyed, frozen by the sight of their bleeding co-worker. I shoved the wounded man into the first office, and straight-armed another who stood dumbly at the door.

"Lock this door, shove the desk up against it and get on the floor," I screamed. "Do it!"

I slammed the door shut and ran down the hall waving people back to the offices and urging them to block their doors. They moved like zombies, sluggish from shock. Then a shot echoed through the corridor. The bullet careened off the floor and ploughed a deep furrow in the wall, and office doors began slamming into place. At the end of the hallway, there were no more offices. The only door led to the fire escape stairs. I heard my name called out and froze. Sidney's voice was deep and sepulchral. The hair at the back of neck tingled, and a shiver crawled down my spine.

"Brandt," he said. "I'm disappointed in you, Brandt."

I turned. Sid's gaunt face reminded me of the death head skull worn by Nazi SS troops. The hideous smile stretching across his face was all teeth and sinew. He walked slowly toward me, the AK loose in his hands, his head moving side to side.

"You disappoint me, Brandt," he said. "I thought you of all people would understand. You don't though, do you?"

"No, I don't, Sid," I said. "Let's stop the shooting and talk about it."

It was a stupid thing to say and Sidney's ghoulish laugh made sound even dumber. When he finished cawing, Sidney frowned and shook his head.

"Too late," he said simply. He raised the rifle and took aim.

I grabbed the handle of the fire escape door and threw it open just as he fired. The bullet sounded like a sledgehammer as it banged into the heavy steel door and slammed it shut. The door caught me in the back and sent me sprawling onto the stairs. Pain shot through my spine and legs, nearly paralyzing me, but the adrenalin pumping through my veins got me to my feet and started me running up the stairs two and three at a time. My footsteps rung like church bells through the steel reinforced stairs. I reached the next landing and kept going. The door below banged opened and I felt another shiver run down my back as Sidney's voice bellowed up to me like Satan's reaching up from Hell.

"I am *so* disappointed in you, Brandt!"

Sidney fired blindly up the stairwell. The blast echoed off the concrete walls as the bullet ricocheted off the steps, leaving a trail of sparks and flying dust. Another shot buzzed angrily over my head and showered me with powdered concrete as it hit the stairs above. The smell of cordite drifted up the fire escape shaft, mixed with the smell of concrete dust. Then the stairs began their hollow peal as Sidney climbed after me.

"Brandt! There's nothing up there, Brandt. Nothing to stop me!"

As soon as he said it, I knew he was right. The next landing led to the roof exit and probably a locked door. I hesitated, my legs refusing to move and considered backtracking to the last landing. Another shot told me Sidney was already there. I climbed the last few steps, my chest pounding and my breathing coming in gasps.

When I reached the landing, I almost cheered. The door to the roof was a fire door. Above it, a sign warned, ALARM SOUNDS WHEN OPENED.

The alarm shrieked as I burst through it, just as another round from the AK slammed into the door's steel frame. I shouldered it closed and looked around. The roof was flat and covered with graveled tarpaper. It was empty, except for the square hut housing the top of the stair shaft, and a small pile of discarded construction timber. The boards—4-by-4s and 2-by-4s—were dried and weathered, dusty with ash and wrapped in spider webbing that stretched like taffy as I pulled one of the larger pieces from the pile. I shoved one end of the 4-by-4 under the door's handle and jammed the other into the tarpaper roof. Pulling a smaller board from the pile, I leaned against the side of the shaft. My breathing came in short gasps as I gripped the board like a baseball bat and waited.

I didn't have to wait long.

The fire door made a hollow thump as Sidney threw his weight against it. He cursed and fired three shots into the door. They sounded like someone using a sledgehammer as a doorknocker. The 4-by-4 sounded like another shot as it cracked, splintered and gave way. The door swung open with a wounded groan. The alarm continued its awful shriek.

"Brandt, you sonofabitch!" Sidney screamed. His breathing was harsh, raspy, but his voice still held its demonic timber. "You betrayed me, Brandt. Just like the others. It's your time now to pay, Brandt. And you know what they say. *Payback's a motherfuck.*"

I looked around the roof. This was where Jack Sweeney came to find peace, where he ultimately met his end. Did he see it coming like this? Did he try vainly to hide from Roger Sherman? Where? The roof was a flat, empty place with nowhere to hide, the perfect killing field. I gripped the 2-by-4 tighter and scuttled along the wall to the back of shaft.

Even with the alarm shrieking, I could hear the crunch of Sidney's footsteps, his raspy breathing drawing nearer. His shadow loomed on the roof, growing longer the closer he got to the corner of the building. I took a batter's stance and waited for the tip of the rifle barrel to peek around the corner.

I swung like I was hitting a homer out of Jack Murphy Stadium.

The board connected with Sidney's soft gut. The air rushed from his mouth and nose, and he bent double. I drew back on the board and swung again, downward this time, aiming for his neck. But Sidney was quicker than I thought. He stepped into my swing, taking only a glancing blow on his shoulder, and shoved the rifle stock into my own stomach. The board cartwheeled from my hands as I went down on my knees. The blow made Sidney squeeze off an accidental round. It went wild, skipping across the roof with a high-pitched whine. Sidney swung the rifle toward my head, but I grabbed it before he could put a gash on my head to match the scar already there.

For a moment we were frozen in time, glaring at each other over the rifle grasped in our hands, like adversaries staring across a trench line. I was stronger than Sidney and in better shape. But he had the strength of a full rush of adrenalin and who knows what else, the kind of strength that makes normal men lift over-turned cars off family members and turns a drug addict into a Hercules when confronted by police.

I pushed myself to my feet, but Sidney used his shorter advantage and his superhuman strength to push me back until finally the roof wall pressed into my back and there was nowhere else to go but down, like Jack Sweeney. Sidney pressed the rifle toward my throat, his mouth twisted into a malefic grin.

"Sidney, why?"

The words were a harsh whisper through clenched teeth. Sidney leaned in and answered me in a voice that made me cold throughout.

"Someone has to make them pay," he whispered. "Someone has to make them hurt, too." I could smell his acrid breath, the stench of sweat and stale booze on his shirt and in his pores. He was too close and it gave me my chance. I butted my head hard against his face. He screamed and his grip weakened. He staggered backward as I pushed him, blood pouring from a smashed nose and lacerated lip. I was nearly in a position to force him to his knees, to yank the damn rifle from his hands and slam it into his face when I slipped on the graveled tarpaper of the roof and fell. My head hit the wall and sent a jarring pain down my back. Searing flashes of light burned my eyes from the inside. When I open them again, Sidney was standing over me, the AK pointed at my head.

"Don't fight it anymore, Brandt," he said. "Everyone loses once they get involved in this place."

Then he pulled the trigger.

Nothing.

Sidney glanced at the rifle and cursed. I squinted, trying to see past the fireworks blinding me. The AK's bolt was stuck open on an empty chamber. The round Sidney had let loose jabbing me with the rifle stock had been the last of the magazine.

Sidney fumbled with the empty magazine. I willed my legs under me and tried to stand, but there was too much pain and not enough strength left in my limbs. Besides, I wasn't certain anymore which way was up. The magazine fell with a clatter and another slid into its place. The bolt snapped with a metallic click, then Sidney lowered the rifle again.

I heard the shot, deeper and throatier than normal, but felt nothing.

Sidney turned violently to his right, a stunned expression on his face. The AK let go two rounds in quick succession, higher pitched than the first. The slugs pounded the wall to my left. I rolled to my right, away from the wild firing. Another shot, like the first, and Sidney bucked forward and landed at my feet, two gaping holes in his back oozing blood.

The fireworks in my head cleared enough for me to see Jo standing behind Sidney. She had gone back to Sherman's office and found what she had been looking for, what I had forgotten. Now she stood in a crouch, arms extended, smoke streaming from her 9mm army-issued pistol.

Her eyes had lost the cold anger they held earlier. Now they were darker, deeper set, and empty.

CHAPTER 26

Sherman was right. There was no way they were going to let me publish the Stanning story.

The police had arrived by the time Jo half-carried me down from the roof. Fire fighters and paramedics were triaging Sidney's victims, separating the wounded from the dead. The floor where Sherman's office was located was rank with the wet copper smell of fresh blood. The toll was eight dead, including Sherman, Godzilla and King Kong, and, of course, Sidney Clipper. There were four wounded survivors, including the phony CID man.

Then there was Jo.

A balding police detective dressed in faded jeans, a white shirt open at the collar, and a corduroy jacket questioned her and me at length about Sidney's death. We used one of the empty offices. The door had three holes in it that were not part of the original design. Three corresponding holes pocked the opposite wall. No one had died here, thank God.

Jo sat in a chair behind a large desk in one of the empty offices, her blonde bangs stuck to her forehead with sweat. I stretched out on a sofa in the office, my head still spinning, my back aching. The detective was polite, and that made me nervous. He was just tying up loose ends, he explained. Sidney's death was obviously self-defense. Justifiable homicide.

He had just one last question.

"Can you tell me, Miss Rice," he asked, "why did you have a gun with you in the first place?"

Jo looked at the detective and I looked sharply at her. She plucked at the hair drying above her brow. Her eyes were still hollow blue globes.

"I'm the Pentagon's security liaison here," she said, as if the answer was obvious. "I have access to all varieties of classified information. I'm authorized to carry a weapon at all times."

The cop seemed to accept that. He grunted, scribbled in his notebook and muttered: "More spooks." Afterward, he arranged for a black-and-white to take us to the hospital. We stayed there the night, Jo treated for shock, me for a mild concussion and a bruised spine. In the morning, they arrived.

"They" consisted of two men, one short and thin, with a receding hairline and round yuppie glasses resting on a long, thin nose perched above a thin slit of a mouth. He looked like a cross between a CPA and a lawyer. The other was big and dumb-looking, like a cross between Godzilla and King Kong, and obviously brought along for physical intimidation. The shyster carried one of those expanding file holders and it was packed. They said they were representatives of the federal government, but they offered no names or credentials, even when I demanded them.

"Mr. Brandt, we need to know what Colonel Sherman told you before he, ah, died," the shyster said.

"Who said he told me anything?"

"The gentleman that was with Colonel Sherman when you arrived said the colonel spoke to you and Miss Rice at length before the, ah, unfortunate event."

The shyster's glasses exaggerated his eyes. After thinking a bit, I decided he looked like a darker Sidney Clipper.

"Now what did the colonel tell you, Mr. Brandt?"

"He confessed to a variety of criminal actions," I said, sighing. "Among them, illegal shipment of weapons and technology, treason, aiding and abetting the enemy during a time of war, illegal possession of drugs and, finally, a couple counts of premeditated murder. It was sort of a death bed confession, only he didn't realize he was about to die."

Neither the shyster nor his muscle liked my attitude. I could see it in the look of distaste on the shyster's face. The big guy frowned menacingly at me. I blew him a little kiss.

"I hardly think you categorize Colonel Sherman's actions accurately," Mr. Brandt," the small man said. "Everything he did was under the color of law."

"Everything he did was extra-legal and you know it. Maybe we should let the readers and Congress and the courts categorize them," I said.

"I don't think we will."

The shyster reached into his expanding folder and removed several file folders. Each had my name typed on the tab. Some had TAX YEAR followed by dates under my name. Another file was stamped DEA. Another had nothing but my name.

"No, I don't think we will bother your readers nor our legislators and judges with this matter."

"You can scare off one magazine, but I doubt even you and Bubba here can scare off the entire U.S. news media," I said. "I'll find a market."

I considered about telling them I had already found a market with Michael Larrs, but thought better of it. One of the few wise moves I had made in recent weeks.

The shyster pursed his lips and gave a shrug.

"It has been done, Mr. Brandt," he said. "History is replete with instances when the American press has been scared away from stories—or at least subtly steered cleared from them. But I don't think we need to go to such lengths in this case."

He selected half a dozen of the largest files and tossed them on the hospital bed beside me. I glanced through them, then laughed.

"You're trying to scare me with a tax audit?" I said. "That might work with someone who earns enough to make tax cheating worth it, but I don't. Besides, I have an accountant who does everything for me. He'll testify—"

It was the shyster's turn to laugh.

"Mr. Brandt, did I say those were the returns you actually filed?"

His lips formed a thin cruel smile as I flipped through the returns. They bore my name, my signature, my accountant's, too. But the dollar amounts were way out of whack.

"These aren't my returns," I said dumbly.

"Exactly, Mr. Brandt," the shyster said, still grinning. "But only you, me, my colleague here, and a half dozen, um, specialists who prepared these returns know that. Once they replace the originals, no one at the IRS will ever know the difference. Certainly the federal judge who tries your tax evasion case wouldn't know the difference."

"We could fight this." I said it, but I didn't believe it.

"Of course, you could, Mr. Brandt." The shyster pulled another file from the stack and tossed it on the bed. It was the one marked DEA. "But at the same time, you might also have to fight charges of drug smuggling stemming from your relationship with certain known members of Latin American drug cartels."

I scanned the DEA file. It made me sound like Carlos Escobar's first lieutenant.

"This isn't right," I said. "The only dealing I had with drug traffickers was as a journalist interviewing sources for news stories. The DEA agents I knew down there knew that. They'd never write this crap."

"But did I say the DEA wrote that report, Mr. Brandt?"

The shyster smiled again. So did his behemoth friend. I sized them up. A man with a small body and another with a small mind, each enjoying their positions of covert power to wreak torment and vengeance on a world they felt had abused them. If my head wasn't still swimming, I would have gotten up and smashed those smiles into the back of their heads.

"Oh, and then there's this."

He held up a manila folder, then tossed it at me. Inside were news clipping from a Palm Springs newspaper about a shootout.

"Three men died in that shoot out, if I recall, Mr. Brandt."

"They were trying to kill me," I said. "They killed my ex-wife and my friend. The cops know all that."

"But let's say a new witness comes forth, Mr. Brandt."

The shyster rose from his chair, slipped his hands into his pockets, and paced the floor.

"A witness who sheds new light on the case, as they say. Someone who would testify in court that you were part of the smuggling operation along with those three men. Ah—" He pointed to the DEA report. "Remember this report now makes you a known cartel associate."

He started pacing again, hands in his pockets.

"And this witness testifies that you sanctioned the murder of your ex-wife and planted the bomb that killed your friend because he was getting too close to the truth. Between this new witness, that DEA report, and those tax returns showing how you laundered certain monies—well, what could a jury conclude?"

The shyster grinned.

"You see, I don't think we need worry about you publishing this story anywhere, now do we?"

I stared at a spot on the far wall and said nothing.

"I thought not."

The shyster collected the folders from the bed and replaced them in the expandable case. He turned toward the door, then stopped.

"And Mr. Brandt, we will be checking on you for a while, just to be certain. That includes your house, so if you have anything that might be problematic to us, I suggest you dispose of it in an appropriate way. Do we understand each other?"

I still said nothing. The two bastards walked to the door and opened it.

"Goodbye, Mr. Brandt," the shyster said. "It really has been a pleasure. For me, at least."

"You're not going to get away with this," I finally said.

"Oh, and why not, Mr. Brandt?" The shyster's eyes were large and amused behind the yuppie lenses.

"Sooner or later, it's going to come out," I said. "Someone else will stumble on it. You have me tied up, but someone else will eventually find out. You can't threaten all the press, no matter what you say."

"Mr. Brandt, listen to me carefully," he said slowly, as if speaking to a stupid child. "Anyone who publishes this story will be landed on by the force of God. And we're God. Good day, Mr. Brandt."

§

They released me from the hospital two hours later and I took a cab back to my bungalow. I don't remember anything of the ride home. My mind was on other things.

Once home, I made a drink, smoked a cigarette from my nightmare stash, and thought. When I finished both the smoke and the drink, I picked up the phone and called Michael Larrs.

"We had an appointment yesterday, Brandt," Larrs said. "Is this how you work, missing appointments?"

"Something came up, Larrs," I said. "Or didn't you hear about the shooting at ConEl?"

"I heard about it," he said. "I also heard you were there again. What's going down over there, Brandt? Does the shooting have something to do with our story?"

"No," I lied. "It was a random act. I was just caught in the middle again. And there is no story."

"What?" Larrs' stage projection was so good I thought I could hear him without the phone. "What the fuck are you trying to pull on me, Brandt? You owe me, remember? You owe for that stunt you pulled years back."

"Sorry, but I screwed up," I said. "The story didn't pan out. There's nothing. No story."

"Brandt, you sonofabitch!"

"And you're right, Larrs. I do owe you. And I will pay you back someday."

I hung up and stared out the window.

"And payback, Larrs," I muttered, "is a motherfuck."

I made another drink, sat back at the desk, and erased all the Stanning note files from my computer's hard drive. After that, I ran a defragmentation program to delete them for good. Then I burned all the print outs in my kitchen sink, and washed the ashes down the drain.

I went to my little hidden wall safe and removed the Stanning lawsuit and the Pentagon report Polmar sent me. I went to the bedroom, slipped on a pair of old gloves, then to the kitchen for a clean dishcloth. Back at the desk, I rubbed down each page of the suit and the report, then slipped them both into a large manila envelope. From the desk drawer, I took Larr's business card, wiped it clean with the dishrag, then used a glue stick to fix it to the envelope. I pulled a long strip off the tape dispenser, wadded it up and tossed it in the wastebasket. I took two fresh strips off the roll, and taped the card more securely. I put more than enough postage on the envelope, and didn't bother with a return address.

I stuck the envelope in the waistband of my pants, then pulled on a jacket even though it was too warm for one. Before leaving, I slipped off the gloves and took a white handkerchief from my dresser. Then I walked to the post office to check my box, checking for anyone who might be following me. No one seemed to be.

Inside the post office, I used the handkerchief to pull the package from my belt and dropped it in the mail slot.

"Payback's a motherfuck, Larrs," I whispered.

EPILOGUE

The quick rap at the door had the sharp precision of a military drill team. I knew who it was before answering it. Jo Rice stood there in full dress uniform, complete with ribbons and spit-shined shoes. Only her face lacked the military crispness she bore the first time I saw her in uniform.

"You look tired," I said.

Jo limped in and took off her beret. "I've been up all night," she said. "Did you see the news last night?"

I nodded. Three days after I had mailed the package to him, Michael Larrs aired the story. As I expected, he did little more than read the Stanning lawsuit and the Pentagon report. By rushing to broadcast, he hadn't alerted the shyster and his cohort.

"It wasn't the full story, though," Jo said.

"No, but it was enough," I said. "It's already in this morning's papers. By tomorrow, Larrs will be on the Larry King Show. All you need is a crack to let in the light. Soon, others will start looking at it, then Congress. That's the way it happens."

Jo put her arms around me. "I'm sorry. I know what the story meant to you."

"He deserved it," I said. I'm sure she didn't understood how I really meant that. Larrs would be in for some powerful retribution from Sherman's comrades. *Payback*.

"I wonder how he got it?" Jo looked at me suspiciously.

I just shrugged.

"You're all dressed up, Captain Rice," I said. "What's the occasion?"

"They're burying Sherman today with full military honors."

"You're kidding. Flag-draped coffin and gun salute?"

"The whole thing." She tossed her beret onto the couch and dropped down next to it. Her face was slack and dark circles surrounded her eyes. "Washington's covering everything up. Everything. Even what Sherman did to Mitch, Alvarez, and the rest. They're going to bury that traitor like he was a national hero."

"You want some coffee?"

She shook her head. "I want you to come with me."

"Where?"

"Sherman's funeral."

I sat next to Jo and put my arm around her. Being intimate with an army officer was getting easier all the time. "You're going to his funeral?"

"I have to stop them," she said. "I owe it to my men. I've been up all night thinking about it, and I owe it to them. I've got to stop them."

"Stop them?" I eyed her suspiciously. "How?"

"Not like that," she said. "Not like I tried with Sherman. That was stupid."

She turned to me, her eyes wide and imploring. "Will you come with me?"

At that point I think I would have followed Jo Rice to hell and back. I nodded and she smiled for the first time since arriving. Then she kissed me.

"Let me get changed," I said.

§

We took my car and headed out toward Point Loma. We stopped at a pawnshop on the way, and I waited in the car while Jo made her purchase. The clerks in the store followed her to the door and watched her get in the car, wondering, no doubt, what the beautiful but crazy army captain wanted with her purchase.

The point road took us past the navy submarine base and a myriad of naval research facilities. In the middle of them was the national cemetery, a sloping bluff overlooking both the bay and the Pacific. It was a beautiful day, and we could see across the ocean to the Coronado Islands. A tiny knot of people and a military honor guard marked the spot of Roger Sherman's last resting place.

I parked a discreet distance away, and turned to Jo. She watched the services for a while, then turned to me.

"You sure you want to go through with this?" I asked. "Have you thought what it will do to your career?"

Jo smiled sadly. "What career, Peter? They've notified me I'm being medically discharged." Her eyes grew hard and cold, the look that gave her nickname. "At least I got my pension."

I just nodded.

We got out of the car. Jo straightened her tunic and checked her pocket. "Stay here, okay?" she asked. I nodded again.

Jo marched straight toward the mourners. The honor guard was at rigid attention. A young airman in a crisp blue dress uniform began folding the flag covering Sherman's coffin. When he finished, he made a smart about-face to present the flag to the grieving widow.

He came face-to-face with Captain Jo Rice.

"Give me that flag, airman," she said.

"Ma'am?"

"You and your men are dismissed."

"But captain—"

"That is an order, airman," Jo hissed. "You are dismissed."

"Yes, sir!" The airman did a quick about-face, quick-stepped to the honor guard and, with Jo watching, marched them several yards away before dismissing them. The young non-com took one last look at Jo, then turned and walked away, shaking his head.

Jo turned sharply toward Sherman's widow. Mrs. Sherman, fortyish, dressed in black with a black hat and netted veil, reached out for the flag. Jo simply shook her head. She turned back to the grave, reached into her pocket, and placed three stacks of silver coins on top of the coffin, one stack for each man Jo lost in Desert Storm. Each stack had ten coins. It cost Jo a small fortune, but she didn't care. She wanted the symbolism. Thirty pieces of silver, the price of Judas Iscariot's treason.

Jo Rice turned smartly about and, without looking at anyone, marched back to the car.

AUTHOR'S NOTE

T his is a work of fiction. However, I based the plot on a number of historical events. Shortly after the First Iraq War — Operation Desert Storm—the news media reported that during the fighting, several American and European companies secretly negotiated with Saddam Hussein's government to rebuild the Iraqi army. Prior to that war, the Iraqis did try smuggling nuclear weapon detonators from San Diego, California, to Baghdad via London. A joint U.S.-British Customs investigation succeeded in arresting the Iraqi agents despite interference from both the Reagan administration and its successor, the first Bush administration. The failure of President George H. W. Bush to react to Iraq's nuclear weapons plot may have emboldened Hussein, leading to his invasion of Kuwait and the subsequent war. The historical events relayed to Peter by the Mossad agent Tygard are, in fact, true. And the unexpected survival of the American mercenary Eugene Hasenfus after he was shot down over Nicaragua exposed the

Reagan administration's illegal arms sales to Iran to finance its illegal war in Central America, the so-called Iran-Contra Scandal.